GREEDY PIGS

GREEDY PIGS

ALSO BY MATT WALLACE

GREEDY
PIGS

MATT WALLACE

A TOM DOHERTY ASSOCIATES BOOK

NEW YORK

GREEDY PIGS

Cover illustration by Peter Lutjen
Cover design by Christine Foltzer

Edited by Lee Harris

A Tor.com Book
Published by Tom Doherty Associates
175 Fifth Avenue
New York, NY 10010

www.tor.com

Tor® is a registered trademark of
Macmillan Publishing Group, LLC.

ISBN 978-0-7653-9319-7 (ebook)
ISBN 978-0-7653-9320-3 (trade paperback)

First Edition: May 2017

For escapists like me who still need a fictional America that somehow manages to be more ludicrous than our real one.

PART I

WEEKLY ROUNDS

STOP ONE: CHINATOWN

Lena hasn't visited Canal Street much since moving to the city. Most of her excursions outside her own neighborhood revolve around collecting ingredients and product for cooking, and she rarely attempts Chinese dishes. She hasn't had any professional call for it, either. The mid-range kitchens in which she and Darren first worked in New York were all muddled American fare. Their brief foray into working on high-end restaurant lines at Porto Fiero largely saw them preparing Italian fusion appetizers (although you never used the word "fusion" around the executive chef).

Bronko pilots one half of Sin du Jour's catering van fleet, such as it is, through the narrow side streets off Canal, rolling over uneven cobbling from another century. The size of the passenger's seat in the commercial van and the chasm of space between herself and Bronko make Lena feel impossibly small.

Outside her window, Manhattan's Chinatown is still very much what it has always been, despite being held in a vise grip by three of the most expensively and newly gentrified neighborhoods in the city: Soho to the north, the Financial District to the south, and, to the west, Tribeca. Sure, there are restaurants that have closed due to rent hikes. There are new hotels and luxury condos rising in the periphery. But between Delancey and Chambers, between East Broadway and Broadway, Chinatown remains the city within a city that was last transformed by the great deluge of Hong Kong immigrants in the sixties and seventies.

The same low-income residents still crew their small family storefronts and occupy their modest apartment buildings. The district has managed to repel the corporate hordes partly because Chinatown still feeds the rest of the city. As much new money as old is spent in its myriad century-old restaurants and on its imported cuisine. Another factor leading to its preservation is that immigrants have never stopped seeking a new life within its borders; they're still arriving from the East every week, and still upholding the traditions and ideals of their predecessors.

But the biggest reason Chinatown has largely resisted the great injection of hipster botulism stretching and smoothing the face of the rest of the city is the same reason the neighborhood was founded in the first place. Chinatown remains Chinatown because of the people who built it and their children who saw it to fruition, because they own the place, and finally and most powerfully, because they want it that way.

Bronko explains all of this to Lena despite the fact she never asked. It's not that she isn't interested; it's simply that Lena is still confused by both the reason for this outing and his half-inviting, half-ordering her to accompany him. Bronko made it clear this wasn't related to an event Sin du Jour is catering. He simply told her to get in the van because he had "weekly rounds" to make and needed her help.

As the old van shambles through the heart of Chinatown, informed eyes can spot the dialect changes as new arrivals flood the district from the rural areas of Mandarin-speaking Fujian province in southeastern China. Lena, of course, can't tell one from the other. The small storefront before which the van finally halts is practically barricaded with angular signs. The Cantonese characters hand-painted on each have been fading into the cheap wood for decades at least.

"First stop," Bronko announces. "Everybody out."

Lena looks behind them at the large cargo space of the van that is mostly bereft of equipment and completely bereft of any personnel besides her.

"Uh, sure, Chef," she says, unbuckling her seat belt.

By the time Lena has hopped down from the passenger's side, Bronko has already trekked around and is

Matt Wallace

opening the van's rear cargo doors. She trots to catch up, just in time to see him grunting as he removes a large cooler from the back of the van and place it as gingerly as possible on the sidewalk.

"What's in there, Chef?" Lena asks.

"Lunch."

Her brow furrows. "Whose?"

Bronko doesn't answer. Instead, he instructs her to grab one end of the cooler, which she does. It's heavy enough to be filled with several cases of beer.

The storefront's interior seems to suck any intruding day-light into its murky, dust-filled corners. It appears to be a secondhand furnishings shop. There are rows of particle-board shelves filled with out-of-box appliances and used cookware. Chairs, not a single one matching another, are stacked awkwardly, even perilously, almost to the ceiling. Several larger pieces of furniture have large handwritten price tags tied to them. Several well-maintained layers of undisturbed dust cover everything.

The place doesn't *smell* like a junk shop, however. That's the second thing Lena picks up on. The scents that assault her nostrils, earthen and bitter and something else entirely that's almost antiseptic. They're not quite culinary smells, and yet they're nothing like anything Lena's nose has experienced in Boosha's other-worldly apothecary back at Sin du Jour.

"What am I smelling, Chef?"

"Nothin' anyone born on this side of the world would recognize," Bronko informs her. "Nobody from the other side of the world born in the last thousand years would either, for that matter."

A strong swell in Lena wants to demand what the hell that means, but she crushes it down. However frustrating she still finds the world in which they operate, Bronko is still the executive chef, and Lena is still Lena. On the line or on a battlefield, she's a soldier. She follows the chain of command.

An elderly Chinese man, perhaps in his late seventies or early eighties, enters from whatever occupies the space beyond the back of the shop. He's wearing a Hall & Oates concert T-shirt from 1977 that appears ready to disintegrate at will on his small frame, twill trousers that are probably from the same era, and a pair of dirty sneakers. A few wisps of steel-gray hair still cling to his spotted, wrinkled scalp. Eyes that are undeniably sharp and shine amber even in the low light stare at them with open skepticism.

"Tarr, meet Mr. Mok," Bronko says, motioning at the small figure, "owner and proprietor of this fine establishment."

Lena opens her mouth to greet him but is unable to get a word out before the old man shoves a finger two inches from Bronko's bulbous nose and begins shouting at him in severe-sounding Cantonese.

Bronko responds by setting down his end of the cooler and holding up his hands in the universal gesture of placation. To Lena's surprise, he also begins speaking what sounds to her admittedly uneducated Western ears like perfectly fluent Cantonese.

She does, however, quickly realize the conversation revolves around her, in whatever language they're choosing to have it.

The discussion ends with Bronko breaking back into English to insist, "Dammit, Mok, I said she's cool, all right? Let it go."

Mr. Mok falls silent, but he's still staring daggers up at Bronko. He's half the head chef's size and twice his age, yet in that moment, Lena isn't sure who'd be left standing if they chose to go at it with fists instead of words.

Fortunately, in the end the old man just nods, once, sharp and final. He turns his fierce amber eyes on Lena.

"Welcome," he greets her, his accent thick but the word deliberate and clear.

Lena finds she can only nod in return.

Bronko flashes her a "your eyes only" look that is drenched in exasperation for the old man, but Lena can tell the pair of them have a long-standing relationship. There's an obvious familiarity there, even a bond. She imagines they go through a form of this exchange every time they meet.

Bronko takes up his end of the cooler and Mr. Mok leads them across the shop and through a beaded curtain separating the front of the store from a back room. It's crammed to the gills with more secondhand junk, everything from children's Big Wheels to home fry cookers stained with petrified grease, and none of it sorted in any particular order, at least to the casual observer.

In the corner of the small cluttered space, four other elderly Chinese people, two men and two women, are seated around a circular wooden table. As Lena enters behind Mok and Bronko, she's immediately intrigued by two things: the first is that all four of them appear to be wearing the exact same Hall & Oates concert T-shirt that Mr. Mok wears, and the second thing is they're all enthusiastically engaged in a board game.

More than that, it's an English board game, something called A Touch of Evil, and judging purely at first glance, it's more elaborate than any of the board games like Clue Lena was forced to play as a child.

There are in fact two full shelves adjoining the corner behind them that are filled with colorful boxes of all shapes and sizes, containing dozens upon dozens of board games. Many are illustrated with Cantonese and Mandarin characters, while others are English editions.

Judging from the size of some of them, they're even more elaborate than the one spilled all over the tabletop now.

The foursome doesn't stir, doesn't even stop play, as Bronko follows Mok into the space. As soon as they become aware of Lena's presence, however, the game immediately ceases and the entire mood of the room changes. One of the couples stands with a spryness defying their advanced years, while the other two turn in their seats, no less at the ready.

Lena isn't sure what she feels in the next moment. It's as if the barometric pressure in the air abruptly shifts, and something like electricity touches the surface of her skin, raising microscopic hairs. It's as if the actual environment in the room has turned against her.

She'll realize later what she felt in that moment was power: power emanating from that table and those people, power attached to an intangible "ready" switch that was suddenly flipped when she walked into their space.

Lena will hope she never experiences that power's "on" switch.

Mok holds up his withered hands, repeating the same word in Cantonese several times. Then, in a loud and careful mockery of Bronko, he gives them two thumbs-up and says, "She *cooooool.*"

The foursome around the table immediately relaxes, and the physical effects permeating Lena's body recede as the air in the room returns to normal.

The Chinese contingent, including and especially Mr. Mok, all laugh, not at Lena but at Bronko.

"Assholes," Bronko mutters under his breath.

The foursome returns to their game, and Mr. Mok apparently doesn't feel the need to introduce any of them to Lena. Instead, he walks past their table to a dark depression amid the wall-to-wall junk. Lena realizes it's actually a small door at the top of a staircase.

The steps are earth-covered stone, lit by work lights hung from the low ceiling and, in the absence of those, old Christmas lights strung along the wall. The stairs descend longer and farther than Lena thinks possible. There are several offshoots along the way, small nooks opening from the side of the staircase into lighted rooms. The trio never pauses long enough for Lena to register more than brief flashes of each.

In one room she glimpses several young people in flowing multicolored robes doing what Lena registers as hand-to-hand combat training. There are glints of light on the steel of weapons, broadswords and Chinese hooks. In another room, the corner of Lena's eye catches the back of a white-haired woman or man's head as they kneel in prayer before an altar adorned with green plants and carved stone.

By the time they reach the very bottom, Lena has

counted over two hundred steps and her breathing has become labored. The air feels a lot thinner wherever in the bowels of the Earth she's found herself.

"You okay, Tarr?" Bronko asks without looking over his shoulder at her.

"Check rog," she answers, trying to filter out the bitterness before it bleeds into her words.

The subterranean chamber into which the staircase opens is more like an elegantly finished basement in a home from the 1970s. The walls are paneled with a dark, richly textured fake wood. Several cabinets and chests of drawers line them. A lush Oriental rug covers most of the laminate floor. It's bare except for a small, ornate table in the center of room upon which incense is burning. Lena smells lilies and something sweet like anise.

"Over here," Bronko instructs her, guiding the heavy cooler across the room.

They place it on the rug in front of a gargantuan, hand-carved bamboo armoire that obscures most of one of the room's walls. Its closed doors are large enough to fit a MINI Cooper. Each side has large Cantonese characters carved upon it.

"Are we serving down here, or—" Lena begins to ask, only to have Bronko put a thick finger to his lips to silence her.

He points to the adjacent wall. Mr. Mok is rummaging

through one of the room's many chests of drawers. As they watch, the old man carefully removes and dons a pure white linen Wudang over his vintage rock T-shirt and trousers. A black-and-gold sash is then deftly slipped over that. He fits a hexagonal hat of dark silk over his small, mottled head and finishes by removing his sneakers and replacing them with soft, pure white slippers.

The last thing he removes from the drawers is a rolled-up rug, which he carries with him and unfurls between Bronko and Lena, directly in front of the armoire doors.

Lena isn't sure whether she's more intrigued or apprehensive as she watches Mr. Mok kneel upon the rug and raise his arms, beginning to recite a deep, almost lyric prayer to some unseen power.

She looks over at Bronko, who smiles reassuringly back at her.

It helps a little.

When Mr. Mok finishes reciting the incantation, or whatever it may be, he motions impatiently at them both.

Lena again looks to Bronko for a sign of what to do. In answer, he gestures at the doors of the armoire, grasping the handle of the one closest to him.

Lena does the same, gripping the handle of the door on her side. When he gives her the nod, she pulls it open. It's heavier than she would've thought, and Lena actually has to use her other hand to help move it the rest of the way.

An inhuman squawking greets them all as she and Bronko push the doors aside, and Lena quickly realizes the armoire houses a terrarium of some kind. She also immediately sees that the armoire is just a façade, and the glassed-in enclosure it conceals recedes far back into the wall of the room, as well as high above the ceiling. It's an entire cavernous hollow beneath the street into which someone has built a small window. The cavern is filled with cane stocks and lush green foliage, dripping with moisture from a top-of-the-line irrigation system erected throughout the habitat. Dark, flat, craggy rocks have also been planted in the soft soil that fills the bottom of the enclosure.

The creatures are the size of small ponies. They're mostly birds, except for sections of their sleek bodies that appear armored, almost like turtle shell. Shining gold feathers with splashes of fiery red cover the majority of their bodies, including their long necks and dagger-shaped wings. Long, hooked beaks the same orange-speckled brown of their exoskeleton dominate their small skulls, each one topped with strands of flowing red plumage that fall across disturbingly human eyes.

There are two of them, grooming each other lazily there upon the rocks. One is slightly larger than the other, but beyond that small difference, Lena would be hard-pressed to tell them apart.

Upon spotting Bronko, they leap down from the rocks, squawking merrily, and press the curved tips of their beaks to milk saucer–sized holes in the glass separating them.

"Larry and Mary, my Chinese eagles," Bronko greets them warmly, letting them nip affectionately at his fingertips through the glass.

"Not eagles!" Mr. Mok insists. "And that not their names! I tell you every time!"

"Welp, until you give 'em names, they seem to like Larry and Mary just fine," Bronko tells him, undisturbed.

"Not the place of mortals to name them!"

Mr. Mok follows the brief tirade by launching into a stream of angry, accusing Cantonese.

Bronko ignores him, looking at Lena.

"It's feedin' time."

Lena nods. She'd deduced that much by now.

"What are we feeding here, Chef?"

"Fenghuang," Mr. Mok answers for him.

Lena just blinks at him. "Okay, but that doesn't really help me—"

He gestures grandly to the birdlike creature on the left. "Feng!" Mok declares, enunciating slowly and exasperatedly as if to a small, slow child. Then, sweeping his arms toward its counterpart: "Huang!"

"Boy and girl," Bronko explains. "Or, y'know, male and

female, if you wanna be literal. They're known as the Chinese phoenix. Only no fire."

"*What are they*, though?" Lena asks, her own patience bottoming out.

"Protectors."

"Of what?"

Bronko takes a deep breath, then shrugs. He seems at a loss.

"Balance, I guess. I'm just a li'l ol' hick from Beeville, Texas; the higher mysteries of Chinese spirituality and whatnot are slightly above my pay grade."

"Right," Lena says. "A hick who speaks fluent Chinese."

"Spent three summers workin' the line at the Fragrant Lotus Garden in Houston. You soak in more than that moo shu smell, y'know?"

"Uh-huh."

"Long ago," Mr. Mok begins, speaking more quietly and with more compassion than Lena has yet heard in the old man's voice, "fenghuang, sacred, divine, protect my people from yaoguai."

Lena looks at Bronko.

He waves his hand. "Like . . . evil spirits. Demons."

"And agent of yaoguai," Mr. Mok adds, irritated. "Fenghuang serve light, serve balance. Fenghuang keep balance here on Earth."

"Why 'long ago'?" Lena asks.

"They were hunted to near-extinction," Bronko explains.

"By who? Or what?"

Bronko's lips tighten. It's almost as if he's afraid to answer that question.

"Pandas, mostly."

Lena's eyebrows shoot up. "Pandas?"

Bronko glances uncomfortably at Mr. Mok.

"Yeah," he says, tentative. "Pandas. Y'see—"

Lena can't help it, nor does she even try. She bursts out laughing.

"Come on, Chef. Seriously. You're talking about pandas? Black-and-white, nibbling bamboo—"

Mr. Mok suddenly springs to his feet. "Panda agents of pure evil! Panda most vile creature ever walk the Earth!"

"Don't start with the panda thing," Bronko practically pleads with him. "All right? It's not her fault. She doesn't know. She's not saying—"

"None of you know!" Mr. Mok rages. "All you do, you ignorant gweilo, you go to zoo and take a picture of a panda with your phone. 'Awwwwwww, the panda ate the bamboo! The panda make a sneeze! I post a video to YouTube! Get so many likes! Panda so cute! So sad they gon' be extinct. Must protect the panda!' Cannot name one Chinese province, but evvvvvvverybody in America know panda. Panda, panda, panda!"

Mr. Mok curses for thirty full seconds in Cantonese then before finally stabbing a finger of ultimate judgment at Lena.

"I tell you this!" he practically spits at her, seething. "Panda make fool of you *all*!"

As he continues to explode, Bronko leans in and whispers to Lena. "Apparently, pandas were engineered to kill fenghuang like our friends Larry and Mary in there. A big-ass war ensued. Most of Larry and Mary's kind were killed. Ditto the pandas. The ones that lived are kind of like Nazi war criminals and I guess our zoos are like Argentina. They hide out there behind an impenetrable wall of public relations, and as long as they keep actin' cute, they're untouchable."

Bronko turns back to Mr. Mok, speaking loudly but politely above the old man's continued rant.

"Mr. Mok! May we please feed the sacred beings now before your admittedly justified screechin' causes them to starve?"

That alone seems to quench the fire in the old man. He turns away from them and kneels, beginning to roll up his prayer rug.

"Panda War great and terrible," he mutters to himself. "Panda War last centuries. Kill millions. But no *Wikipedia page,* no happen. Only thing worse than panda is *Internet.*"

Cursing quietly, he pads across the room to return the rug and his other ceremonial garb to their proper place of storage.

Now that the initial shock of the information has worn off, Lena begins to feel guilt knotting her guts. She wants to apologize to the old man, but the strictly rational part of her brain still clinging to basic truths of the "real" world before Sin du Jour simply won't allow her to even form such an expression aloud.

Bronko hunkers down with a grimace. Lena can hear the bones in his knees pop. He opens the cooler. Half a dozen foot-long cylinders of thick stainless steel are arranged atop cold packs. There are small, clear slits running along the side of each cylinder. The tubes inside are filled with a murky liquid, and as Lena looks down at them, she can see dark shapes clearly moving through that muck.

"Dare I even ask, Chef?"

Bronko half-grunts and half-chuckles. He grasps one of the cylinders and holds it up to her.

Unafraid, Lena takes it from him and examines the small window into the tube more closely.

"Is it . . . an eel? Or a snake?"

Bronko stands, holding another one of the cylinders in his hands. He carefully fits the top of it against the hole in the glass habitat. On the other side, the fenghuang begin bobbing up and down on their thin legs and pronged feet, tittering excitedly.

"Both and neither," he tells her. "Just like Larry and Mary here ain't exactly birds. They're all things from a time of legends, a time that don't exist no more. Makes ordering takeout a helluva thing, y'know?"

He depresses a button on the side of the cylinder that pops the end cap open. A slick, dark spear of scaly flesh lances from inside the tube and goes slithering off across the rocks.

The fenghuang whip away from the glass and spring into the air, soaring low over the rocks and through the foliage, after it.

"They like to hunt," he explains to Lena. "It's part of the whole deal. A regular ol' snake wouldn't last half a tick."

"So, where do you get . . . Chinese phoenix food?"

"I don't," he says, taking the cylinder in her hands and readying to release its occupant into the habitat. "Ritter and the team rack up a lotta frequent-flyer miles tracking them down."

Inside the habitat, Larry and Mary have pulled apart their first course and Mary is hot on the tail of the one Bronko has just released through the glass.

"So . . . this is like a takeout service Sin du Jour provides?" Lena asks, watching them. "How does he afford that, selling thirty-year-old toasters and crap?"

"There's no charge," Bronko says, chucking an empty cylinder and readying another.

Lena looks away from the creatures inside the habitat, staring up at him, confused.

"But this has gotta cost a freakin' fortune. Does Allensworth—"

Bronko laughs, loud and hard and sour.

"Allensworth wouldn't piss on either one of these things if they were on fire. He ain't exactly the conservationist type. Not to mention the Chinese he works with are probably the ones who bred the damn pandas in the first place."

It takes Lena a moment to process it all, and she still comes up short.

"So, what? You front this? Yourself?"

Bronko nods.

"Every week?"

He nods again.

"Why?"

"Because if we don't do it, no one will. And Larry and Mary in there'd just . . . waste away. Now, they ain't the last of their kind, strictly speaking. I know of a few other places like this, none of 'em local. But . . . it's gettin' close for 'em. And there's no place left for Larry and Mary except the ones people like Mok make. The world, our world and the one we serve crab cakes and terrines of whatever-the-fuck too, both those worlds have moved on, and they've left behind . . . as Mok over there'd call 'em . . . creatures of light and balance."

Lena doesn't know what to say, not to any of that, but the implications of his words are like a barbed weight on her chest.

Bronko just watches her, waiting.

A moment later, Lena bends down and picks up the last cylinder. She turns and angles it carefully against the hole in the glass, popping the cap and releasing Larry and Mary's final course into the habitat for them to enjoy.

Bronko grins.

As they pack up the empty cylinders in the chest, Mr. Mok approaches them, again clad in his street clothes.

"You have many questions," he says to Lena.

"I, uh, I guess so," she replies, not sure what else to say.

The old man nods. "To feed fenghuang is a holy thing. A sacred thing. You take on that responsibility now."

Lena's eyes dart to Bronko, then back to Mr. Mok. "I'm just helping out—"

"You have questions," Mr. Mok continues, ignoring her. "If I can answer for you, I will. You may come to me with your questions."

"Wow. Okay. Thank you."

Mr. Mok doesn't respond. He merely stares at her, as if waiting for something.

Lena looks to Bronko.

He shrugs. "I think he wants you to ask him a question."

"Oh. Okay," Lena says, inhaling deeply. "All right. I . . . Okay, I've got one. What's with the Hall & Oates shirts?"

Bronko has to stifle his laughter.

Mr. Mok squints at her very seriously. He holds up a single, withered digit of his right hand, the gesture almost reverent.

"Hall & Oates *number one* rock and roll *forever.*"

Lena nods very slowly. "I see. Got it. Thanks."

Mr. Mok nods with a sharp grunt, moving past them to close the doors of the armoire.

Lena's expression as she peers up at Bronko must be asking another question, something like "What the *actual fuck*?"

He only shrugs. "Ancient Chinese wisdom right there, man. You gonna argue with it?"

HEAD OF THE CLASS

Darren crosses the Brooklyn Bridge in the Dodge Neon he and Lena have shared for so many years, neither of them can now remember who actually owns it.

The address Ritter gave him is somewhere in Brooklyn Heights. Darren was obviously disappointed when Ritter told him he'd be too busy to continue training Darren over the next few months, but Ritter took the time and care to make Darren understand Ritter wasn't blowing him off. He told Darren he'd found a temporary replacement instructor for him, and that training with someone new would help Darren far more than it would hurt him.

Knowing—or at least suspecting—the kinds of people (humans or otherwise) Ritter would refer him to for training actually has Darren excited.

He finds himself pulling up to the curb in front of a dilapidated brownstone. That's not so odd, but the fact that it also seems utterly forgotten does strike Darren as just short of a miracle. There are no construction vehicles or equipment attached to the place. There's no signage indicating it's for sale, or has been sold, or will soon be the site of luxurious new condos. It's sitting in the middle of a vibrant, rejuvenated street, yet the building has been left to age completely unimpeded.

There should be realtors bleeding each other in the yard for control of such a property.

Darren leaves his car parked and treks across the brief dead patches of ground just beyond the brownstone's rust-crippled gate. He double-checks the address and finds it's the same one Ritter jotted down for him. That old, familiar impulse to flee the uncertain before he embarrasses himself fires up inside Darren, and his conscious mind stomps on it with a soccer hooligan's fury.

He refuses to be afraid of people anymore, let alone a spooky-ass building in Brooklyn Heights.

Finding the front door unlocked, Darren confidently lets himself in. Ritter told him he'd be expected at this time, and expected is exactly how he's choosing to behave.

The place has been completely gutted. There aren't even dividers between floors. At first, Darren wonders if he's early for some sort of fight club. That's what the space reminds him of with its bare, stained concrete floor, industrial columns and rusty steel beams standing out against the shadows of the high, dark ceiling.

"Is anyone in here?" he calls out, answered solely by the echo of his own voice. "My name is Darren Vargas.

Ritter told me I'd be starting training here today. I work with him at Sin du Jour."

No answer, not even the flutter of pigeons in the high beams or rats scurrying in the walls.

Darren takes out his phone, ready to call Ritter and at least verify the address. He's cursing himself for not at least asking Ritter more about what the hell he was supposed to find here. Taking people he looks up to totally on faith is an old Darren move.

The mirror wasn't there just a brief second before, and nothing Darren's rational mind attempts to con him into believing can or will change that fact.

It is there now, a seven-foot pane of reflective glass held in a simple black iron frame.

It's just standing there, in the middle of the ground floor, erected to perfectly face Darren as he glances up from his phone.

"Okay," he says, just to hear something besides silence as he stares at his reflection in what he is already determined *not* to think of as the ghost mirror.

It's just him looking back. He's trimmed back his beard because James was starting to complain, and sculpted it into a slight V shape because Darren loves how it looks on Denzel Washington's son in that HBO show *Ballers*.

"Is this, like, a test?" he calls out. "Is it magic? Like that Harry Potter mirror. Or is it—"

His reflection actually changed several seconds before, but it was so subtle, it took him until this moment to realize *how* it has changed.

Darren is no longer looking at himself as he is now; he's looking at himself as he was several months ago. His beard is gone. His high-and-tight haircut has reverted to all those oil-slicked dark strands he used to cultivate, trying to look like a Tejano pop star. His body is just a little softer; the definition he's earned through training practically every day is gone.

It's more than simple grooming choices, however.

It's that stupid, frightened look he always used to wear.

It's all summed up in his eyes and in that placid, perpetual smile that begs to be liked, or at the very least not victimized. His eyes are desperate, cloying, even terrified.

That look is plastered on his face, and it's all the Darren of now can see.

All he sees is the version of himself who watched helplessly while his best friend was about to be killed by a monster.

All he sees is the Darren he's been working every day for months to kill.

"You fucking pendejo," he says to that Darren, the one who never spoke Spanish, who didn't want to sound "too Mexican" because he'd been hardwired to believe he'd never rise above busboy that way. "You fucking weak pendejo. Look at you. Look at you!"

His reflection doesn't speak any of those words. Darren's reflection, his old self, stands mute. The curses and disdain being hurled at him causes that Darren to physically crumple, just a little, but enough to make him appear exactly as weak as his new self accuses him of being.

"Stop it!" Darren orders his reflection. "Stop that crap now! Stop it, you pathetic piece of shit!"

His reflected self tries, but the tears begin to roll over his cheeks. It's just two thin streams at first, but once the floodgate is broken, he begins crying full-on.

The disgust that churns in the pit of Darren's stomach as he watches his former self cry is a feeling unlike anything he's ever experienced. He feels as if he's no longer looking at a person, a human being evoking empathy and basic decency. Darren is looking at a thing, a loathsome subhuman thing unworthy of even the simplest compassion.

"You're nothing," he says to his weeping reflection in a voice no one who knows Darren would recognize. "You're less than nothing."

That empty, bottomless disgust turns. It becomes fury. It becomes an all-consuming desire to destroy the weak, pitiful thing staring him in the face. The Darren staring into that mirror, at that abominable version of him, is shaking. He can barely control his limbs. His lips peel back over his teeth like an animal growling at prey.

In the next moment, he's lunging, diving at the mirror, into it, through it.

The glass shatters, but Darren's reflection is not obliterated. The shards rain down harmlessly, evaporating like raindrops on a steaming street. The black frame of the mirror simply melts into the shadows surrounding it. The mirror is gone. What's left is that weeping Darren in the flesh, and he falls under his snarling, enraged present self with a shriek of fear and pain.

The Darren of now straddles his past self upon the dirty concrete and begins hammering fists down into his face.

Darren on top doesn't realize tears are now pouring from his own eyes, angry, hot tears mixing with the spittle flying from his snarling, cursing mouth.

He beats that perfect replica of his face until it's unrecognizable, not only as him but as something human. He pummels it until the muscles in his arms and shoulders burn from the exertion of it, until he's gasping for breath and his knuckles are split and bleeding and throbbing with pain. He finally stops when he can't feel anything under his fists anymore. He holds up two trembling, brutalized hands that are totally gloved in viscous red and dripping with gore.

What they've left on the ground beneath him barely has a head.

Shaking, Darren rolls away from the near-headless form, flopping hard onto his back. He's sobbing uncontrollably now, holding his battered fists against his body, curling around them as he convulses and retches. The thunder in his head and the torrent in his guts are a storm that lasts for centuries, perhaps longer, wrecking him to his core.

What's left in its wake is a shell. When the blood has finally stopped flowing, when the tears and mucus have all dried up, and when the howling ceases, the only thing Darren feels is hollow. The rest is totally numb.

He doesn't know how long he stays curled up there on the floor, alternately staring at the grain in the concrete and the darkness inside his own eyelids.

When he thinks he'll just stay there forever, lie there until he becomes part of the floor, petrified and beyond the veil of human feeling, in that moment, a voice finally answers him.

"That ... was just lovely," the voice says, made of smoke and reeds and spoken through sheer silk. "You've already far exceeded my expectations. Usually, it takes days to hollow out a potential sword. But you, sweet boy, are ready to begin your training right now."

STOP TWO: (Underneath) 57th Street & 7th Avenue

Bronko and Lena catch the Q train on Canal and ride it to 57th and 7th. Lena usually enjoys the train, the motion and the time to herself, even if that last part is often interrupted by some rando who doesn't understand headphones and a book are popular international symbols for "leave me the fuck alone."

This particular ride, however, and her enjoyment of it are both hampered by the fact they each have a fifty-pound leg wrapped in wax paper slung over their shoulders. They're also carrying their individual knife cases, and Bronko has a thermal satchel slung from his opposite shoulder.

"What did these legs come off of, Chef, a T. rex?" Lena asks, somewhere beneath Times Square.

"Ram," Bronko answers.

Her eyes somehow manage to bulge and narrow at the same time.

"These are *ram* legs?"

"Yep."

"Like, a dude sheep?"

"Yes'm."

"Where the hell are there rams with legs this big?"

"Nowhere anybody vacations nowadays."

Lena just shakes her head, shifting her steadily weakening frame under the giant appendage. Her next question is obvious, but then, she realizes, so is the answer to that question.

"Ritter?" she asks flatly.

Bronko nods.

"They get around, don't they?"

"That's their job."

"Has anyone in Stocking & Receiving ever died doing that job?"

Bronko sighs. "Tarr, folks die doin' every job there is. Crab fisherman or cubicle worker, it just takes one really fucked-up day."

"So, does that mean 'yes'?"

"It means there's a lotta implied context in your tone I don't rightly agree with, and I'll thank you to let that be the final word on the subject."

"Yes, Chef," Lena says, without sarcasm.

"Thank you."

They disembark, carrying their giant cones of carefully folded wax paper like a very fastidious caveman and cavewoman. Instead of walking across to the subway exit,

Bronko leads Lena down the warning-yellow edge to the very end of the platform. Her steps slow as she watches his broad back begin to descend the unseen access stairs that lead into the subway tunnel.

"Chef?"

"Just c'mon," he instructs her. "We're not servin' in the station."

"Yeah, this seems much more sanitary, Chef," Lena answers back, voice trembling just a little.

She reluctantly follows, her pulse racing and her glance moving suspiciously all around her, and she proceeds to violate every rule of subway patronage by trespassing beyond the platform. No one stops them, but she almost jumps as she spots, in the darkness below, a worker in MTA coveralls and a safety helmet and vest. He's watching them descend. Lena's body stiffens beneath her burden and adrenaline causes her veins to beat against her skin like the paddles of a pinball machine.

To her surprise—and immediate relief—the worker simply nods and gives a half-salute to Bronko as they pass in the tunnel below.

They follow a cement ledge several feet removed from the subway tracks, a few dull orange safety lights occasionally throwing their shadows against the wall, but otherwise they walk in darkness. Lena isn't sure how far; she knows only that she's following the back of Bronko's chef's smock like some great moving wall of white standing out against the pitch.

"I think this is it," she hears Bronko mutter, more to himself than to her.

Lena stops walking. "You *think*?"

"There ain't exactly street numbers down here, Tarr. C'mon."

Bronko rounds a corner Lena didn't even realize was there and quite literally disappears into the wall of the tunnel.

She finds herself jogging frantically to catch up with him, not wanting to be left guideless in the dark. She bounds around what turns out to be a narrow slit cut into the wall, almost like a smaller access tunnel. She spots the white of Bronko's smock and follows it through the cramped space to where it ends in an equally cramped iron door.

"Ha!" Bronko triumphantly proclaims. "I was right!"

He pushes open the door with a great protesting shriek of grinding metal and ducks inside.

Lena follows, careful not to scrape the product over her shoulder against the walls or doorframe.

It's some kind of disused workers' quarters, or at least it appears so to Lena at first glance. There are cots draped with drab olive blankets and flattened pillows in the corners. Rows of small square lockers line the walls. A maroon patina has overtaken patches of the lockers' original metal, but they seem to have suffered solely from age, not neglect. There isn't a millimeter of dust covering any surface in the space. You'd almost have to describe it as clean.

Five bow-legged wooden stools surround a communal table in the middle of the quarters. There's another angular table shoved up against one wall, beside a cracked porcelain sink. Not far from that is an old wood-burning stove with a pipe as thick and heavy as a small tree trunk running from its potbelly into the low ceiling of the quarters.

"So, is it time to ask who or what we're feeding?" Lena asks.

Bronko hefts the ram's leg from over his shoulder and onto the tabletop near the sink. He places his knife case and thermal satchel he's also carrying beside it.

"Trolls," he casually informs her.

Lena practically slams her ram's leg down on the table beside his. "Trolls?"

Bronko nods, opening his knife case.

"Trolls."

"All right, then," Lena says, and asks no more.

She finds she's become comfortably numb to receiving this kind of information.

"Butcher that big sumbitch," Bronko instructs her. "Big-ass strip cuts, thick as you like."

"Yes, Chef."

Lena unzips her knife case and removes her largest, sharpest filet knife. She carefully unwraps the large, raw piece of ram and sets to work breaking it down.

Watching Bronko butcher meat is like watching a master surgeon perform an operation in a battlefield tent. His hands move with urgency, faster than she can keep track, but also with mechanical precision that defies such speed.

Lena works far slower but no less meticulously. While her cuts take four times as long to complete as Bronko's, each one is machine-perfect.

When they're finished, Bronko unzips the thermal satchel and begins piling nearly three-feet-long, thoroughly cleaned femur bones between the cuts of meat.

"Do you have a cleaver?" he asks her.

Lena half-grins. "Don't you, Chef?"

In answer, there's a whisper of metal kissing nylon and Bronko unsheathes a razor-sharp meat cleaver with an ergonomic handle.

Lena quickly realizes the handle bears Bronko's name and it's actually from his own line of cutlery.

"I asked you, Tarr."

Lena nods, reaching into her knife case and retrieving not a meat cleaver but an actual full-sized camping hatchet.

"Jesus," he says. "You and Cindy should really hang more."

"We've been trying to, actually."

"I guess nothin' brings women in an office environment together like a succubus ensnaring all the men in said office and trying to murder everyone."

"Most of us, anyway. Have you talked to Jett since all of that went down? She was pretty fucked up."

Bronko only nods, offering no further comment on the subject.

"Break these fuckers here down lengthwise," he says, referring to the femur bones. "We're going to roast and extract the marrow."

Lena doesn't question him or the massive size of the bones. She simply sets to work hacking through the centers of each, using a small steel mallet from her knife case to strike the back of the hatchet after each initial cut. She separates the bones vertically into three-foot halves.

As Lena prepares the femurs, Bronko is shoving wood into the hundred-year-old wood-burning stove and starting a fire in its iron belly. While he waits for the flames to catch and consume the wood, Bronko busies himself prepping the ram's meat. He coats every inch of each steak with a spice rub of his own creation.

"Straight salt for the marrow, Chef?" Lena asks him.

Bronko nods, and she sets to sprinkling aggressive

amounts of salt over the fatty marrow inside each exposed half of femur bone.

When the fire's stoked to a temperature that suits Bronko, they begin feeding their prepared product into the furnace to cook.

"I hope we're feeding a platoon," Lena remarks.

Bronko snorts. "Something like that."

They come shambling in forty-five minutes later, as if drawn by the smells filling the subterranean lair. Lena hears the first one before she sees it, as the creature is forced to violently stuff its own frame through that tiny iron doorway.

Trolls look a lot like nightclub bouncers from New York City in the 1970s. Their eyebrows are competing with their scalp in a never-ending volume contest while the hair on their chests and arms battles for third place. They're all over eight feet tall, with gargantuan torsos, short bowed legs, and thick, knotted arms that literally drag their knuckles against the ground as they walk.

"Smells like Saturday," the first one through the door says in a voice so deep and garbled, it might be coming from under water.

Bronko laughs as he begins pulling smoking meat from the smoldering iron confines of the furnace stove.

"Tarr, this is Hongo. Hongo, this is Lena Tarr. She's helping me with my rounds this week."

"Hope you cook better than this *puhtruhumph*," Hongo says, and whether the last word is a pejorative in his own language or just chomped-up English, Lena isn't sure.

Four more follow him. Each troll is clad in ragged overalls. Their feet are bare and crusted as hard as granite. Hongo is pulling two large burlap sacks behind him, one of which is beginning to soak through and leave a viscous trail on the floor. One of his compatriots is carrying what looks like a makeshift battleaxe, a chewed wooden club with the end of a roadwork sign driven horizontally through one end. The metal sign, which reads BUMP, has had its octagonal edges filed and serrated menacingly.

The trolls crowd around the table in the middle of the space, and Lena can't deny there's a comic joy in watching them all balance their gargantuan selves atop those tiny wooden stools.

"How go the wars, boys and girls?" Bronko asks the room at large.

A chorus of weary grunts and groans and a brief, fearsome growl answers him.

"Wars?" Lena says, low enough to keep between the two of them.

Almost as if in answer to her question, Hongo slams one the bags he's carrying onto the tabletop. Its contents spill out, a mixture of MetroCards and small coins Lena realizes are discontinued subway tokens. The other bag he flings expertly and almost without thinking into one corner, where it hits the wall with a wet splat before half-sliding, half-falling into a large plastic trash receptacle.

"A lot of folks," Bronko explains, quietly, "just plain regular human folks, live down here in these tunnels, y'know. There's practically a whole other city underneath our city. Nobody up there cares. Nobody's lookin' out for 'em. They're forgotten. Think about everything you've seen, Tarr. What d'you imagine most nonhuman races would call a dark, enclosed, underground city filled with people nobody topside cares about or will miss?"

"A buffet," Lena says immediately.

Bronko nods, stacking medium-rare ram steaks and bone vessels containing beautifully caramelized roasted marrow several feet high atop an ancient cast-iron skillet with the circumference of a car windshield.

"Think of trolls like the World Wildlife Fund, only humans who live under bridges and in tunnels are the wildlife."

With that, Bronko hefts the skillet and carries it across the room to the communal table, dropping it like a bomb on the center of the tabletop.

The five trolls set upon the feast as if it's still held inside the body of living prey trying to evade them.

Bronko just manages to step clear of the feeding

frenzy, returning to the furnace, where he begins tamping down the fire.

Lena folds her arms, leaning toward Bronko as she watches the quintet devour the meal she's helped prepare.

"I thought . . . in the story . . . the troll under the bridge was the bad guy and the rams were the good guys."

"Rams are dumb animals, Tarr," Bronko assures her. "And they're assholes."

"And the MTA . . ." she trails off.

"They pay the toll. Besides Allensworth, transportation authorities are probably the most well-versed governmental-type body when it comes to the netherworld. And trolls are big-time hoarders. Doesn't much matter what, gold or worthless tokens. But they still gotta eat. And it's not exactly like they can head up to Union Square and hit Taco Bell."

"Does the MTA pick up your tab?"

Bronko shrugs. "I invoice Allensworth. The fuck does he care?"

"So that means we're on your time right now, Chef?"

He nods. "And yours. Is it worth it?"

As Lena looks on, Hongo shoves half the length of a roasted ram's femur in his mouth and snaps the bone in half with no effort, crunching it between his massive, snaggletooth jaws.

"There was a time I could've ended up living down here, with those people you were talking about."

"So, that's a 'yes?'"

Lena nods.

"Good!" Bronk pronounces. "Glad ya feel that way. You're on cleanup. I'm tired."

He laughs at the look she shoots up at him then, deep and genuine, and it's the first real bout of laughter she's seen possess her executive chef in months.

To Lena, it's a sound more than worth scrubbing down a few dirty pans.

CAKES AND LITTLE BOYS

Nikki loves baking as much for its simplicity as for the challenge of it. There's a very clear structure to what she does, a precision to which she must adhere to see the desired outcome. Cooking is chaos, or at least it has always seemed to her. "Improvisation" is just another word for not having a plan. She can't conceive of how chefs ever plate a dish that way. Baking is a science. When you improvise science, shit explodes.

Also, sometimes when you use liquid nitrogen, shit explodes, but she maintains the rest of the staff exaggerates that incident.

In the small pastry kitchen that is her domain, Nikki is a monk perfectly duplicating manuscripts. That's where her laser focus serves her best. She follows the recipe for her black pepper strawberry cake to the tiniest corner of the letter. She believes eating fondant is as redundant and flavorful as performing oral sex on a plastic blow-up doll. Nikki uses a piping bag filled with a frosting of Jamaican Blue Mountain coffee and chocolate she made herself, a spatula, and a small sculpting tool. That's it.

The exterior of the finished product is as smooth as silk draped over steel, and the lines of her frosting designs are so flawless, they might be machine-pressed plastic.

Fucking fondant, she thinks to herself as she licks the spatula.

She's come into Sin du Jour on an off Saturday to bake cakes for a family party. Nikki bakes in her home often for personal occasions, but for larger jobs, she doesn't see the harm in using the company's equipment. She's baked birthday cakes for her seven-year-old niece and her friends, and larger cakes for the attending adults.

"Nikki? You back here?"

It's Dorsky's voice, no mistaking it.

Nikki freezes, accidentally squeezing a stray dollop of frosting from the piping bag onto the cake.

"Shit, shit, shit!" she seethes as quietly as possible, waving her spatula-wielding hand in frustration.

"Nikki?" he persists, and she can hear him approaching the entrance to the kitchen.

"Yes, dammit, I'm here!"

Dorsky walks into the pastry kitchen. He's not wearing his chef whites, which makes him look somehow odd and out of place. But he's also not wearing a jacket in January weather so he can show off his biceps, which makes him look exactly like Dorsky.

"I stopped by your place," he says. "I figured I'd take a

shot you were here doing your thing. And I had some expense reports to turn in, anyway."

"You stopped by my place?" she asks, almost alarmed, but it's not enough to pull her focus from removing the errant frosting and patching over the blemish on her cake.

"Yeah, I needed to talk to you. *Need* to talk to you, I mean."

"About what?"

Nikki uses the sculpting tool to smooth the raised remnants of the frosting she spilled and blend it into the rest.

"There," she whispers to herself. "Perfect."

"About something that's been on my mind since all of that crazy shit went down with the Enzo Consoné gig."

Now that the cake is fixed, Nikki's full attention is brought to bear on what he's saying, and it's enough to make her raise her hands in a panic.

"Tag, before you say anything else, can we both agree my engaging in happy fun time with you strictly to break you free of a succubus's spell is a self-explanatory kind of situation that doesn't require further discussion? Like, ever?"

Dorsky just blinks at her in silence for a moment. When it comes to anything that doesn't relate to cooking or the business of running a kitchen, Nikki knows his wheels turn about half as fast.

"What, that?" he finally says. "No. That's not what I want to talk to you about."

"Oh. Oh, okay, then."

Nikki sounds surprised, and then disappointed.

"I mean, did you want to talk about it?" Dorsky asks, cautious.

"No!" she insists immediately. "No, of course not." An impatient, vexed air overtakes her. "What do you want, Tag?"

"Right. I just . . . I feel like I owe you an apology."

Nikki's impatience quickly turns to sheer bewilderment. She doesn't even know what to say to that.

Realizing she's not going to help him along with it, Dorsky quickly continues. "The whole thing with what's-her-fuck, Luciana, the way you all . . . you and Lena and Cindy and Jett, I mean—"

"The womenfolk of the office," Nikki clarifies.

"Yeah. The way you had to deal with that on your own, and the way you were shut out of the kitchen—"

"Lena was shut out of the kitchen. I've never been very welcome there."

Dorsky sighs. "All right, yeah, fair, so I owe you an apology for that, too. My point is, you stepped up for the line in a big way when we'd all turned on you, and you shouldn't have had to do it yourselves. Evil fuckin' snare-bitch or not, I feel like . . . like maybe I made it easy for her to divide and conquer us. I was pissed at Lena for taking off without so much as a voice mail, and I was pissed at you for being on her side when she came back, which is stupid, I know."

"It is. It is *very* stupid."

"I get that. And as long as I'm apologizing, I might as well go all the way back to what happened with us . . . before. I liked being with you, but I didn't treat you so good when we weren't alone."

"You treated me like Danny Zuko when he first saw Sandy again in *Grease*."

He furrows his brow at her. "Is that the play or, like, the movie? I've never seen—"

"Never mind, Tag. Why . . . What brought all this on? Seriously? This is the most un-Dorsky-like behavior I've ever witnessed, and that includes when you were under the total control of an evil she-demon."

He looks genuinely frustrated, and it's that more than anything he's said thus far convincing Nikki he may be sincere.

"I don't know. I don't . . . I don't want to be that guy who talks a bunch of shit about who they are and then fails spectacularly to live up to it. That guy raised me. Fuck him. I always tell myself, and everyone else, the line means everything to me. I'd do anything for my line.

More than that, I call myself a leader of that line. I haven't been living up to any of that lately. You and Lena have. You've done more than your share for this place. You deserve better. You deserve better . . . from me."

"Wow" is all Nikki can say at first. Then: "Well. Thanks. I mean it. Thank you. That is shockingly mature of you. And I appreciate it."

Dorsky nods, seeming at least slightly appeased.

"Can I have some of that cake?" he asks.

Nikki giggles. "Yeah. Sure. I think you've earned cake."

As she sets about cutting him a healthy slice, Nikki asks, "What about Lena? Are you going to have this talk with her?"

"Yeah, I need to," he admits. "It's just . . . there's going to be more to say with her. It's more . . . complicated."

"Like an adult relationship?"

"I'm not the dumb jock in a John Hughes movie, Nik; I know what sarcasm is."

Nikki slides a plate in front of him with a wedge of cake and a fork on it.

"So, what are you going to say to her?"

"I don't know," Dorsky says, forking an inhuman-sized bite and somehow managing to fit it all inside his mouth.

He says something else, but the words get lost amid the layers of frosting and crumbs being broken down between his jaws.

"What was that?" she asks.

He swallows. "Where is she at with Ritter?"

Nikki frowns. "That's not a question to ask me, Tag. It's none of my business."

"I just want to know if it's even worth bringing up all the other stuff, or if I should just say I'm sorry like I just did and leave it at that."

"Ask Lena, and then you'll know."

"It's not that easy."

"It's always that easy. People are just dumb."

Dorsky cuts another forkful and relishes the bite.

"This cake is fucking awesome."

"Of course it is," Nikki confirms without hesitation. "I made it."

STOP THREE: THE WITCHES OF WILLIAMSBURG

"Hey, this is my neighborhood."

Lena recognizes her favorite Chinese takeout restaurant, Family Garden, on the corner before noticing they've turned onto Metropolitan Avenue.

Bronko grunts as some sort of basic acknowledgment that a fact has been stated in his presence.

"Good Ecuadorian joint around here, I recall," he mutters a moment later.

He double-parks the catering van in the middle of a block only five up from Lena and Darren's apartment building. Bronko hits the hazard lights, ignoring a horn blast from a dry-cleaning van careening past his window.

"This'll be a quick one," he assures her. "There's a cooler behind your seat. Grab it and follow me."

He reaches behind his seat and with a grunt of exertion, hefts a large open box up onto his lap. Lena glances inside as Bronko reaches for the door handle. The box is filled with various sundries and dry foods. Lena realizes it must be for a home filled with women. She spots tampons, sanitary napkins, "lady" shaving razors, and several other hygiene products made specifically for women.

Before she can question him, Bronko has left the pilot seat of the van. Lena opens her door and climbs down from the passenger seat. She needs both hands to pop the handle and pull apart the side cargo door, and it strains her considerable forearm muscles in the process. The cooler behind her seat is of the large Styrofoam gas-station variety, although knowing Bronko, it's filled with dry ice and who knows what kinds of product.

Lena fills both arms with the cumbersome object and lifts it out of the van. "What's in the cooler this time, Chef?"

"Vacuum-sealed entrees and sides, mostly. Ya got some of my vegetarian tequila and lime risotto balls. Got some nice Jack-and-cherry-glazed tri-tip I stayed up all night doin' at home. And, o' course, Mama Luck's own bacon-and-turnip soup. All ready to be sous-vide and served."

"Is this for some kind of tapas bar for the homeless or something?"

"Not hardly. Think of 'em as Chef Luck's Extra-Fancy *Teeee-Veeee* Dinners."

For the last sentence, he puts on his hammiest performance voice, as if he's back on his old cable cooking show.

Lena can't help laughing.

"C'mon," he bids her.

They're standing in front of a small art supply store, but rather than lead Lena inside, Bronko walks over to the lowered ladder of the building's fire escape beside the storefront.

"Chef—"

"No talkin'," he hisses at her. "Just do what I do and follow me back to our ride."

Bronko, with surprising speed and grace for a man of his bulk and advancing years, trots up the rungs of the ladder, assisted only by one hand as his opposite arm is occupied with the box. Bronko stops short of ascending onto the first fire-escape balcony. Instead, he hoists the box through the opening in the black steel grate and slides it directly beneath a closed and gray-curtained window on the second story.

Descending halfway back down the ladder, he reaches out to Lena silently for the cooler. She offers it up, expression curious even as she remains quiet, and Bronko takes it from her easily. He's up the ladder, depositing the cooler beside the box, and back down again in less than ten seconds. As soon as his booted feet hit the pavement, he pushes the ladder back up into its cradle above the sidewalk.

"It's kind of a safe house," Bronko informs her as they climb back inside the van.

"Like, for battered women?"

"Witches."

Lena blinks.

"Excuse me?"

"Witches," Bronko repeats, staring past her, through the passenger window at the fire escape where he left their special delivery. "Real ones, I mean. None of that Internet Wiccan crap. The *Sceadu* and Allensworth's people regulate the hell out of 'em. You can only practice as part of a licensed coven. Witches without covens are called 'solitaires.' They're illegal, leastwise in America. They're hunted down. And worse."

Lena, horrified, looks out her window and up at the fire escape. A moment later, the curtains part, the window there opens, and slender, tattooed arms extend to pull the box and the cooler inside. They quickly slam the window shut and draw the curtains.

Lena frowns. "If Allensworth hunts them, why does he let you do this?"

Bronko shrugs, starting up the van. "I assume he knows and lets it slide. What does he care? He's a big-picture kinda guy, after all. If it keeps the wheels greased and the machine runnin', he'll let us feed a few solitaires holed up in Williamsburg."

Before they pull away, Lena's eyes are drawn to another window, this one on the third floor. The curtains part and Lena can just make out a very small, white face, wild tendrils of stark white hair framing it. She sees the dot of a fingertip touch the glass and begin to spell something out in the thin sheen of dust there.

Then it's all gone, left behind as the van pulls forward and rejoins the metallic blood flow of the city's veins.

"You're a helluvan extra-worldly philanthropist, Chef," Lena says a few blocks later.

"Oh, that back there?" he asks. "That's not me. That's Ritter. He asked me as a favor to front it. Covers it all outta his pocket; just doesn't want 'em to ever see his face."

Lena feels a lump swelling in her throat.

"Why is Ritter sponsoring a shelter for runaway witches? And why anonymously?"

Bronko shrugs. "You'd have to ask him that. Not my business."

By the time they return to Sin du Jour, it's the end of the day and Lena feels drunk.

"You do this every week?" she asks Bronko as they roll through the waning industrial blocks of Long Island City.

He grunts. "If I didn't, wouldn't nobody else do it."

Lena settles back into her seat, staring out through the windshield. The city looks like a painting hung on a bent nail, somewhere very far away.

"Why did you bring me along this week, Chef?" she finally asks.

Bronko parks the van next to its twin on the curb in front of the red brick fortress that is their company headquarters. As he reaches for the key in the ignition to kill the engine, he pauses and looks over at her.

"Couple reasons, I suppose. I want you to see ... to know ... that there's more to what we do than what you've seen so far. We dance with the devil, sure, but we don't go home with Him. Now, from talkin' to Consoné, we know there's a shit storm a'brewing. We don't know when or how it'll affect us, but I need y'all to know that if there's a fight comin', it's not ... it *can't* just be about survivin'. Y'understand? I need you to believe that this place and what we do are *worth* fighting for."

Lena finds she's nodding slowly and involuntarily as he speaks. She stops.

"What's the other reason?" she asks after clearing her throat.

Bronko draws a deep breath and holds it in for a long time before exhaling to answer her.

"I ain't always going to be around, Tarr. Today, we just ran a few errands, y'know? This was all just the tip of a big-ass iceberg. Who's gonna take those reins when I'm gone? Dorsky don't give a shit about anything outside his own kitchen. Nikki, she got the heart, and Lord knows that girl is hard as stale French bread when she needs to be, but she don't wanna lead. Never has. But you ...

you're more like me, if you won't take unkindly to the comparison."

On the contrary, few words spoken to Lena through-out her life to this point have meant as much as those four.

"I don't know what to say to any of that, Chef," she says, determined to be as honest as possible with him, even if all she can offer is confusion and uncertainty. "None of this is . . . easy. It's not one thing, with one side."

"And it ain't never gonna be," he assures her, firmly but gently. "All you can decide is whether or not it's worth doin'. That's all. That's what I did."

She nods, accepting that.

"Anyway. It's Saturday night and you're still young enough that means something. Thank you for puttin' in the overtime and riding shotgun with an old man."

Bronko climbs down from the van. Before he shuts the door, he leans back inside, looking at her.

"Hopefully, we have some time yet," he says. "Hope-fully, we'll just get to cook a while and be like a regular ol' line in a regular ol' kitchen."

Lena's grin is as bitter as baker's chocolate.

"That'll be the day, Chef," she says.

PART II

ALL ENEMIES, FOREIGN AND DOMESTIC

THE RESULTS ARE IN

The vintage Triumph, noisy as hell and vibrating like something barely tethered to this plane, ducks down the alley and pulls up to Sin du Jour's service entrance. Lena kills the engine and heels the kickstand, leaning the bike to rest directly across from Ryland's ancient RV. As she dismounts, Lena marvels at the brand-new tires on the hulking beige ruin, not to mention a complete lack of city-imposed boots on those tires. It's also missing its protective sheen of petrified mud, as if it's been newly washed (or more likely decontaminated).

Ryland is reclining in a Hello Kitty lawn chair he must've purchased either because it was the first one he saw or the cheapest or both. He's wearing a plastic baseball helmet, the novelty variety with cup holders and built-in rubber straws. Those straws have been cut and elongated with additional tubing and duct tape to accommodate two tall glass wine bottles settled precariously into the cup holders.

The second-generation alchemist has had to Mac-Gyver a chin strap for the helmet out of more duct tape to stabilize it against the additional weight.

"I never thought I'd say this," Lena admits, "but it's good to see you and that roach coach back here where they belong."

"Aye. I'll have you know I've no tolerance for infestation, besides which nothing that isn't me can live in this roving poison farm, and that's merely because I've been accruing an immunity to said poisons since boyhood."

She can barely understand him due to the fact that two rubber tubes filled with wine and a lit cigarette are all jammed simultaneously in his mouth, but Lena gets the point.

"Right. Well, welcome back, Ryland."

Lena undoes her chin strap and stashes her motorcycle helmet beneath one arm, walking up to the service entrance door.

"Would you like to go out with me sometime?" he calls after her. "I've begun studying the Kama Sutra in earnest."

"Sure," Lena shouts back at him. "You settle yourself into position fifty-nine, the sloppy crab, and I'll join you later."

"Truly?" Ryland asks, surprised.

The slamming of the back door answers him.

There's a staff meeting in the kitchen in five minutes, but Lena wants to make one quick stop first. She trots through the winding, seemingly directionless and architecturally impossible corridors, still shocked she half-knows where she's going.

She hears the distinct rattling around and barely audible recriminations before the door to the apothecary is even within sight. Lena finds Boosha in the middle of restocking her high shelves of curios, books, pots, pans, and items that defy human description. The ancient woman has almost gotten the place back in order again, no small feat considering it looked as though a hurricane had rolled through after Allensworth's succubus attacked her.

Boosha speaks quietly to each inanimate object as if it were a wayward child before stowing it away.

Watching her makes Lena smile.

"You are coming here for something?" Boosha asks without turning away from her work.

Lena blinks. She's slightly startled but quickly shakes her head.

"I just wanted to see how you were doing, first day back and all."

"My home is a shambles!" Boosha squawks, gathering her many ragged skirts and climbing down from the steep stool atop which she'd been perilously leaning.

"Yeah, I know. We would've cleaned up for you, but everyone was kind of afraid to touch your stuff or put it back in the wrong place."

Boosha nods, grunting. "As it should be."

Her green-tinted face with its offset features looks almost fully healed. There are still a few light bruises, but none of it seems to have slowed her down.

"I'm glad you're okay," Lena says. "And thank you for your help when you were in the hospital. Leaving that book out made all the difference."

"You would have managed without me," Boosha assures her. "You are smart girl. You will be good leader when your time comes."

"I . . . What do you mean? When my time comes for what?"

Boosha waves her off impatiently, bending to pick up more displaced paraphernalia. "When time comes, you will know for what. Now off with you. Have much work to do here."

Lena sighs. She wants to press Boosha further, but she knows better by now.

"Welcome back" is all she says in the end, leaving the ancient creature who is not quite any one discernible race to her tasks.

The first thing Lena sees upon entering Sin du Jour's main kitchen is Dorsky and Nikki, standing shoulder to shoulder against one of the gas ranges, laughing about something.

It feels slightly like walking into an alternate reality, a

subtle one where everything else is the same except all people wear cheese boxes instead of shoes.

Lena walks up to them, arms folded across her chest. "This must be one universally funny joke."

Dorsky stares at her, immediately lost. "Huh?"

Nikki's smile doesn't disappear, but it does noticeably fade. "No, uh . . . we were just . . . you know . . . talking about everything that's happened lately. Trying to see the funny side."

"Hey, can I talk to you after the meeting?" Dorsky asks Lena.

She nods, feeling even more off-kilter now. "Yeah, sure."

The rest of the line cooks are spread out around the kitchen. Lena takes a place next to James, who is sitting alone at one of the prep stations.

"Where's Darren?" she asks him.

He doesn't quite frown, but Lena can see it takes effort to hold his smile. It's difficult for Lena to picture James without that smile; he wears it like armor, and the optimism and outlook that accompany it are as central to who he is as his faith. He might as well be shedding tears in that moment.

"I do not know," James says. "We rode in to work together. He has been . . . very quiet. And he dreams . . . terrible dreams. He will not say they are, but I see it when he sleeps."

"Training with Ritter isn't helping anymore?"

"He does not train with Ritter. Ritter has become too busy. He sent Darren to a friend of his in Brooklyn, to continue learning."

Lena does frown, and it's deep with concern. "Well. It can't be that mess with that succubus bitch bugging him. You two weren't even here when it all went down."

"Yes, I know. I feel bad, but that was a good vacation."

Lena smiles. She reaches up and pats him on the arm. "I'll talk to him, okay?"

James nods.

Bronko's heavy footfalls and the clacking of Jett's high heels make an uneven chorus, but it announces the duo's presence before they appear beneath the arch separating the kitchen from the corridor outside. Bronko doesn't seem any less burdened lately, but at least he's present and taking care of himself again. Jett, on the other hand, is back in top form, killing it in her finest Chanel suit and tallest Louboutins.

Lena finds herself smiling warmly at the sight of the pair of them. She can't help feeling comforted by their return to form.

Bronko's first question is "Where's Vargas?"

"He is in the bathroom, Chef," James pipes up quickly. "He was not feeling well this morning."

"You're a bad liar and it's a shitty habit besides, James,"

Bronko tells him. "I'd avoid picking it up."

"Yes, Chef."

"Y'all can fill him in later. So, here it is. This mornin' I got the news our good friend Enzo Consoné has won the presidency of the *Sceadu* and we'll be serving at his inauguration in one week, down in some sacred spot in rural Virginia."

The line applauds, catcalling and hooting, some of it exaggeration and some of it genuine.

Lena doesn't know quite how to feel about that announcement, any of it. The last time she and Bronko spoke with him, Consoné told them there was a war coming. She knows his being elected president of the most influential governing body overseeing and mediating all these intersecting supernatural races and powers on Earth (and possibly beyond) will only escalate the situation. Consoné is an independent, a perceived human, and not the one Allensworth wanted sitting at the head of that table.

"At least the shadow election went better than the shit show on CNN," Dorsky comments.

Nikki shakes her head sadly. "I cannot believe he's the new president of the United States. I just can't believe it."

"Speaking of which, isn't that the same night as, you know, the other inauguration?" Dorsky asks.

"I don't even wanna get into that," Bronko says. "It's

done. Take heart in bein' among the few humans who know the American president and all his cronies take their marchin' orders from—"

"Demons?" Lena interjects.

"More rational authorities," Bronko responds, each word a slow, rumbling warning to her.

"I can't speak to the nationally televised inauguration," Jett chimes in brightly. "However, the inauguration of the *Sceadu* president is going to be an event unlike any Sin du Jour has ever planned. I'm reaching beyond my usual channels and workforce, and I can promise you all a spectacle untold!"

The line seems far less enthused by that.

"What about the menu?" Dorsky asks.

Bronko inhales and exhales with equal measures of ennui. "Yeah. I ain't exactly a creative fount lately, I'll be honest with y'all. Suggestions? Thoughts? Level 'em up."

Lena speaks immediately and without really even thinking about it. "It's a menu for politicians. What about an all-pork theme?"

They all look at her, even Nikki, surprised and quizzical expressions on their faces.

Bronko, however, grins. "I like that, Tarr. I purely do. Not bad. Not bad at all."

"That's pretty damn funny," Dorsky admits. "But I like it for the food, too. Pork has a lot more versatility than you see in this city. And most chefs wouldn't have the balls to serve five courses or more of pork. I'm in."

"It won't make dessert easy," Nikki points out, her nose slightly crinkled.

"You're always up to the challenge, Nik," Bronko assures her. "Let's go with it. Tag, you and Tarr there draft a menu and have it on my desk by the end of the day."

"Yes, Chef," Dorsky and Lena reply, almost perfectly in unison.

"The goblin guests will need to be taken into consideration," Jett points out. "However, I believe the rest of the guest list should respond favorably to pork as a theme."

"Pork and gemstones!" Bronko announces with an almost sadistic glee. "G'luck figuring that one out, folks."

Laughing, he turns and exits the kitchen. Jett waves excitedly to them all and follows him.

"All-pork?" Nikki asks Lena. "How'd you come up with that one?"

Lena shrugs. "I'm Hungarian. The only thing we love more than pigs is government satire."

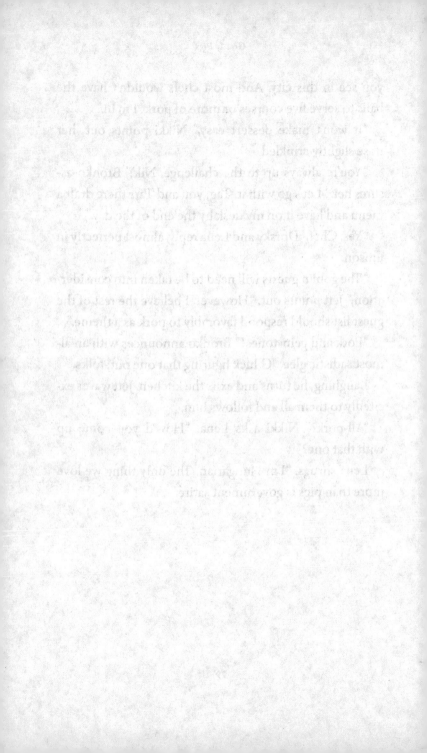

IN THE HOLE

Stocking & Receiving is quiet, just a cement-lined hole in the earth forgotten by all. The team is out of its spacious, dingy "offices" and Darren is making use of the solitude and Ritter's heavy bag, hung on a rusty chain from the ceiling. The only sound, every 6.4 seconds exactly, is Darren's taped right foot colliding with the center of the bag. He rotates his hip, kicks, and recovers methodically and mechanically, over and over again.

He has no concept of how long he's been down here or how many repetitions he's performed at this point.

Darren pauses, standing perfectly still in front of the bag. When he's not in that brownstone in Brooklyn Heights, his mind enjoys a blissful, perfect blankness. It's a fog that protects him from the rest of the world, from seeing or hearing or truly experiencing too much of it.

Still, there are flashes. There are stray moments, like this one, when he becomes aware of his surroundings, of the people connected to them and him. That awareness clashes with the reality he's learning in that brownstone. The familiar surroundings throw that other reality into sharp relief, exposing it for what it is.

In this moment, Darren remembers everything, the mirror that wasn't a mirror, the voice that was all around him until it crawled inside his head and became something else, and all the things it's been showing and teaching and whispering to him since. . . .

He launches another kick. He doesn't move any faster, but this one has an unnatural amount of force behind it. When his foot and shin hit the bag, the bag busts its chain and goes sailing in a perfectly straight line. Traveling at least fifteen feet and as fast as a runaway oxcart, the bag explodes, raining sand down on the floor of Stocking & Receiving.

Darren stares at the stripped cloth and grains of sand flittering down the wall. As he watches the sand tumble, the blankness returns to him, a thick pall cast over his mind that drives away all those troubling thoughts and all that painful awareness.

It's just fine. You don't want to wear yourself out, an inner voice that's not his soothes him. *You have training tonight, after all.*

"Darren! You down here?"

That voice is coming from outside of his head, and hearing it only sends whatever's left of him recoiling further back inside himself.

Lena pushes through the prewar door to Stocking &

Receiving, halting when she sees him standing there in his workout shorts and athletic tape.

"Jesus, dude, what are you doing? I've been looking all over for you. You missed the staff meeting."

Darren doesn't respond. He seems to be catching his breath after a rough training session.

"You okay?" she asks.

"I'm fine."

Lena looks past him, seeing the mess of the heavy bag against the wall.

"What happened there?"

"It broke."

"Yeah, well, don't fuck with it. I'd be amazed if everything down here didn't require you get a tetanus shot. Now, you want to change into your whites and get on the line? We're catering Enzo Consoné's inauguration and we're working on recipes for the menu."

Darren's eyes alight at the brief mention of the new *Sceadu* president's name.

He nods.

"Okay, then," Lena says, still eyeing him suspiciously. "Move your ass, okay?"

She leaves.

Lena's been gone for almost a full minute when Darren repeats, "I'm fine."

PROVERBIALLY

"You wish me to what now?" Ryland asks them, one eye perpetually shut against the afternoon sun while the eyebrow of the other shoots up in confusion.

Lena and Dorsky are standing just outside his trailer, looking in. The Irishman is rooting through the filthy kitchenette of his recreational vehicle, searching for a fork. Perched on his right palm is a plastic bowl of tepid ramen noodles. His functional alcoholism precludes him from eating large or frequent meals, but even he's aware he has to sustain himself somehow.

"It's an idea we had for the *Sceadu* inauguration we're working," Dorsky explains. "The theme of the menu is pork, but we still have to feed the goblins who are coming. So, we were thinking you could, like, literally turn a sow's ear into a silk purse, and we'd fill it with gems for the goblins to eat."

Ryland halts his utensil hunt, staring at him with both eyes open now.

"You know, like the saying? You can't make a silk purse out of—"

"Yes, it's a rather advanced idiom for you, Dorsky," Ryland says. "And I didn't peg you as much of a reader, either, if we're to be totally honest, love."

"He means you," Dorsky informs Lena sarcastically.

Lena ignores them both.

"You know, if you just walk five feet to the building and come to the kitchen, I'll make you whatever you want," Lena tells Ryland, staring at the microwave noodles with open contempt.

"Thank you, no. I've no use for the pretensions and frivolity of what you do."

"Fine," Dorsky says, "but what about the purses? Can you do it?"

"Not only is it an imbecilic notion of the highest magnitude, it is an abject and insulting misapplication of both my skills and the entire craft of my profession."

"Noted," Lena says. "Now, can you make the damn things or not?"

Ryland bends at the waist and grips his legs, muttering too low for them to make out the words, which he's speaking between his ankles.

Lena and Dorsky wait.

When Ryland unfolds himself, he does so with the bellow of a church organ to which angry football hooligans have taken an axe. He stares at them with such weariness in his eyes, one might think there's wisdom there if they didn't actually know the man.

"Bring me the bloody pig ears and I'll turn them into whatever you want; just leave me be now so that I may ingest and then violently regurgitate my supper in peace."

With that, he kicks the door to his RV closed, shutting them out.

"He is such an asshole," Dorsky says as they both turn away from the RV.

Inside, they can hear clattering and glass breaking and Ryland cursing in what might or might not be English.

"So, what did you want to talk to me about?" Lena asks as they walk slowly back to Sin du Jour's service entrance.

"Right. Yeah. That. I . . . wanted to apologize."

Lena stops, looking up at him with even less understanding in her eyes than Ryland received.

"Yeah, I know; I'm getting that look a lot lately," he says.

"You don't owe me anything, Tag. Everything we did—"

"No," he interrupts her. "Not about that. Not about anything that happened between you and me. I feel like we were on equal footing there. I just mean . . . if I made you feel unwelcome in the kitchen, on the line. If I closed ranks on you, I mean. That's not the kind of chef I want to be. I'm trying to do better than that. I told Nikki, too."

"Oh. All right."

Dorsky can't tell if she's surprised or disappointed or both.

"So, we're cool?" he asks.

She nods.

"Good." Dorsky takes a deep breath. "So, about the other stuff—"

Lena holds up her hand immediately. "Can we not?"

"I just want to say. I was pissed when you took off, all right? I was. But you didn't owe me anything. You still don't."

"I know that. But I'm glad you do, too."

"So, how about we just start over again, as two chefs on the line? Go from here?"

"Yeah. I can deal with that."

"Cool."

"I am surprised you pulled that silk purse line," Lena says, changing the subject as they walk back inside.

Dorsky laughs. "I read it on a napkin in this British pub in Manhattan."

THE FOURTH WORLD

"This is a place of the deepest power," White Horse tells his granddaughter. "It is like a natural psychopomp, conducting and guiding spirits between planes as a conduit. It is older than ancient, more potent than any magic. This is the place we'll begin."

"Hey, y'all," the elderly woman in her blue vest and nametag greets them. "Welcome to Copy Kings Max Plus Express. Can I help you find something today? We're havin' a special on printer ink."

"No, thank you," White Horse replies flatly. "We're fine."

"All right, then; y'all have a good day."

Little Dove stares up at her grandfather.

The word "dubious" doesn't begin to cover it.

"What?" he demands.

"We flew all the way to fucking Arizona to come *here*?"

He sighs. "Okay, look. This is a place of deep power *upon which* a regional chain discount office supply store has been built. Can we move on?"

She grins. "Sure, Pop."

White Horse leads her through the warehouse-sized space with its towering aisles of printers and networked phones and floor-model desk chairs. He stops in the middle of one such aisle, Little Dove long having lost the ability to distinguish between them, and White Horse plucks a large hole-punching device from a nearby shelf.

As she watches, nervous, her grandfather removes it from its box, tossing away the packaging.

"Pop—"

White Horse removes a small bone-handled knife from his belt and punctures the rubber bottom of the hole punch, spilling the sand inside placed there as a counterweight all over the floor between them.

"Hunker down," he instructs her.

"Pop, Jesus, they're going to kick us out of this place."

White Horse dismisses that with an impatient wave of his hand, squatting and sitting down on the floor.

"They don't see us. To them we're already dead, erased. If they saw us, they'd have to acknowledge us and all the bad shit that comes with that."

White Horse removes a few vials of colored sand from inside his jacket, uncorking them and adding the hues to the beige pile he's spilled on the floor between them. He begins forming the multicolored mass into a painting.

Little Dove reluctantly drops to her knees, careful of the miniskirt she's wearing.

"Many of our people believe this, everything around us, is the Fourth World, that we pass through three others before emerging here."

"Do you believe that?"

"I believe the universe has many layers not visible to the naked eye, or—more than that—not conceivable to the human mind. There's power contained beneath those layers, power of those that have gone before, their spirits, pooled together, and those who've yet to emerge here."

"And you're going to teach me to call them the way you do?" Little Dove asks, reluctant.

The old man shakes his white mane. "I don't call them, child."

"But I've seen you—"

"I don't see the layers," White Horse explains. "I haven't for many years now. At first, when I was a boy, I only saw ... not holes in them but glimpses. Those glimpses almost drove me crazy. I tried everything short of stabbing out my eyes with a buck knife to stop seeing those visions. But this is how I was born. And since there was no way for me to stop seeing them, I decided I had to see everything. It was the only way. I learned to annihilate those layers completely. Now, to my eyes, spirits walk alongside these people of flesh. I see planes atop planes, and my mind has accepted and adjusted to it."

"Like how Keanu Reeves sees the Matrix in the sequels?"

White Horse stares at her wearily. "Yeah, sure, *exactly* like how Keanu Reeves sees the Matrix in the sequels."

Little Dove nods. "Okay. Okay, so how do you learn to stop seeing the layers?"

"A lot of folks try a lot of different shit, sweat lodges or peyote or vision quests out in the open desert. Most of the time, all they do is trip balls and hallucinate, pretend whatever they saw was real. And that's fine. They aren't seeking power; they're seeking answers, and most answers come from your own mind, anyway."

"Then how do *you* do it, Pop?"

White Horse raises his arms and begins chanting in another voice, the same deep, otherworldly voice she heard him use to cure the staff of their lust possession. It's that voice from which Little Dove wants to shrink. She feels whatever he's summoning pass through her like electricity. She jumps, goose bumps covering her skin.

White Horse falls silent and lowers his arms just as quickly as he began.

The air around them settles.

"I don't know," he says, casually, as if he didn't just speak with the voice of an angry demigod. "It's like squinting to see a hidden picture. I just let go of this plane and open myself to all others, let them come to me."

"That's helpful, Pop, thanks."

"*You* aren't me. You don't have to do what I do."

"What do you mean?"

"A true hataɫii has no power of their own, not really. We heal. We draw strength from what forces we can summon. But the power doesn't come from us. Understand?"

Little Dove nods, afraid of what he's going to tell her next.

"You're different. What I saw you do when that demon Santa Claus fuck tried to X me out ... that came from you. That came from inside of you. You were born with true power, the kind our people haven't seen in countless generations."

Little Dove begins to feel her entire face and skull trembling. She swallows hard and shakes her head to stave it off.

"You don't know that," she insists.

"I'm afraid I do, girl. I'm afraid I do."

He reaches out and takes her wrist, guiding her hesitant hand to his sand painting.

"I've taught you this already. I've taught you how they must be destroyed when you're done painting them."

"Sand paintings are for healing," she whispers.

"Healing means many things. To heal rage is to create peace. To heal evil is to destroy it. Mostly, these paintings are like this place. They're conduits. This is a tool for breaching those layers we just talked about. The procedure, the way of it, it doesn't really matter.

Because it all comes from the person."

"What do you want me to do, Pop?" she almost pleads.

"I want you to fill this painting with your power and use it to see the way I see."

"I don't know how to do that," Little Dove insists, tears beginning to roll over her eyes.

"That's why you have to learn," White Horse urges her, gently squeezing her wrist. "I'm here; I won't let it get away from you. But this is how we begin."

Little Dove uncurls her fingers and begins sifting them through the sand.

"Think of that moment," he bids her. "That moment the demon came for me."

"I don't want to . . . Please . . ."

"Then you'll always be afraid of this and of yourself. And to live in fear is no life. I'm a fuckup, a junkie gambler, but I'm not afraid of what I am. If nothing else, I will leave you that. Now, see it in your mind, child."

Little Dove shakes her head, but the memory is already creeping around the edges of her conscious mind. She closes her eyes. The lobby of Sin du Jour is on fire. It's filled with cackling, jagged-toothed elfin minions. Her grandfather has been skewered by debris and can barely move. And that hideous, horrifying construct, that demon in the form of a beloved holiday idol, is bearing down on them.

Her eyelids snap back. An impossible wind, like unseen hands, wipes away the sand beneath her fingertips, scattering it until there's nothing left. She feels the drums beating in her ears, and it might be the blood of her own skull throbbing or it might be the sound of time itself splitting apart like a rotten gourd.

She sees plasmatic energy flowing all around them, weaving through the shelves and rafters of the otherwise-ordinary store. It moves through her, and when it does, Little Dove sees flashes of memory, hundreds of memories not her own, spanning lifetimes untold.

Then she blinks and it's all gone.

Her grandfather's voice is anchored by concern. "Little Dove?"

She's breathless, sweat dappling her temples.

She can only nod at first.

"I'm okay," she finally says. "I . . . I saw. I saw it, all of it. For just a second."

White Horse pats her hand gently.

"Welcome back to the Fourth World," he says.

LANDSLIDE

Lena reports to Sin du Jour in the early morning hours. It's a long drive from Long Island City to the Virginia woods, and they have to arrive in time to set up service and cook. The guest list is so swollen, they've had to rent two large moving trucks in addition to their trusted cartoon-cake-logo catering vans to accommodate all the fare and their equipment. The vehicles, loaded late into the night before, are lined up on the street in front of Sin du Jour headquarters.

They're not alone.

Long black sedans, half a dozen of them with windows tinted as black as tar pits at midnight, are flanking the foursome of trucks and vans. Lena spots an equal number of suits wearing sunglasses in the predawn, milling about the cars. They put her instantly in mind of the private security contractors her Army division would often encounter overseas.

Lena finds Bronko standing in front of the open cargo door of one of the moving trucks, overseeing a final inventory check.

"Are we carting food or the president himself, Chef?" she asks.

"What, all the spook vehicles and suits? It's a high-profile, high-security shindig. They're our escorts."

"Feels wrong," she says plainly. "They look . . . wrong."

Bronko grins. "Everything feels wrong to you, Tarr. And that's good. We need that. It keeps us on our toes."

He seems thoroughly unconcerned, and there isn't anything rational or logical Lena can say to change his mind.

She walks away and spots Darren sitting on the stoop in front of Sin du Jour's lobby entrance, head nearly dropped between his knees.

"Yo, zombie boy. We doing any better today?"

"I'm fine," he says mechanically.

"I swear, you say that to me one more time and I'm going to fucking deck you, son."

Darren lifts his head and looks up at her, their eyes locking.

"That would be a mistake," he says.

Lena ignores the sudden chill, the sense that something's seriously wrong. It's still Darren, and an overwhelming part of her can't accept Darren would seriously threaten her.

She tries to play it off. "Yeah, I know. You're deadly now, right? All that training you been doing with whatever sensei Ritter set you up with."

He doesn't say anything to that, dropping his head.

"All right, then," she says. "But if you're not going to talk to me, I'd talk to James. You're sincerely fucking that up, and it's a mistake."

She leaves him there to sit with that, hoping at least those final words penetrated.

When Bronko is satisfied they're good to go, he rallies everyone together like a cattle boss ready to start the big drive.

"All right!" he addresses his line, pulling a small slip of paper from the breast pocket of his smock. "Our security escorts here have a specific procedure and seating assignments in mind for the trip for reasons that I'm sure make sense to them, so listen close. Nikki, you take point in the first van with James and Vargas. Rollo, your big Eastern Bloc ass is piloting truck number one. Rest of the line can pile in with you. Tarr, you and Dorsky are in the second van. Pac and Mo can ride along. I'll follow y'all in the last truck with Jett. The big black cars know where we're going, so just follow them. Simple?"

No one has any questions or concerns, at least that they vocalize.

"Good, then. Let's go feed some folks some pig!" Bronko concludes.

Lena wishes Nikki luck, and she and Dorsky walk to

the second van, Lena climbing behind the wheel. When Lena is in her seat, searching for her seat belt, she sees Sin du Jour's busboys are already comfy in the back. Mr. Mirabel is snoring into his oxygen tubes, fast asleep, and Pacific is rolling a fresh joint.

"Pac," Dorsky warns, "you smoke out the food in here and Chef'll put that out on the tip of your stoner dick."

"I'm just prepping," he assures them amiably. "Just like you guys. And girl. Sorry."

When everyone is seated in their separate vehicles, the caravan slowly cranks into motion, moving like a caterpillar from the head down. As they take to the street, the black sedans begin weaving around and in between the two sets of van and truck, both leading and following the Sin du Jour vehicles, and filling the middle of the procession.

"You want to talk or listen to music?" Dorsky asks her once they're driving.

"You're all about the talking lately," Lena says.

"Is that a bad thing?"

"No. Not necessarily. I guess."

"I feel like y'all are speaking in code," Pacific observes from the back of the van.

"Shut up, Pac," they reply together.

Lena and Dorsky glance at each other awkwardly several times.

Finally, Dorsky turns on the radio and begins surfing channels.

Four hours later, Lena is yawning regularly, ready for another cup of coffee and barely paying attention to their progress when she nearly eats the bumper of the sedan in front of them.

"What the hell is he doing?" she mutters.

The driver in front of her has slowed, nearly burying their tail end in her. Lena opens her mouth to curse again, but her driver's-side mirror is filled with two more sedans, their tail guards, pulling up alongside both the moving truck behind Lena and the van itself. They're all close enough to shave paint and metal from the cargo doors.

"They're fucking herding me onto the exit!" Lena rages.

"Same thing with Bronko and Jett behind us!" Dorsky says, looking from one rearview mirror to the other.

Lena watches the other half of the caravan pulling far ahead of them. "I'm losing the others!"

Out of the corner of her eye, Lena watches the moving truck and van ahead of them disappear into the endless flow of traffic continuing southwest. She's forced to turn onto the next exit and keep following their faceless escorts.

"Call Bronko!" she instructs Dorsky.

He nods, pulling out his smartphone and setting his thumb to work.

"I got nothin'," he announces a moment later. "No signal."

"I'm just sayin'," Pac interjects, "if we were all buzzed, we'd mind what was happening right now a *lot* less."

"Son of a bitch!" Lena curses, gripping the steering wheel so hard, her knuckles turn white.

"Where are we going?" Dorsky asks.

She points out the windshield to the green-and-white placards above.

All the signs ahead of them now read the same WASH-INGTON, D.C.

PART III

TWO INAUGURATIONS

YEP, THAT ONE

"Welp," Bronko says to the rest of them, "this is certainly a perfectly normal everyday thing that happens all the time. Yessir."

They're standing on the western steps of the U.S. Capitol Building, about ten yards from the spot where the next president of the United States of America is to be inaugurated in just a few short hours.

"What in the hell are *we doing here,* Chef?" Lena whispers, urgency in her voice as if they've already committed some terrible crime and are waiting to be caught.

Bronko stares down at the suited Secret Service agents guarding the perimeter. They look to him less like human beings and more like appendages of a single organism, programmed with only the basest of instincts. None of them offered so much as a one-word response as Bronko and his people were led into the city and herded past the high-security barricades.

Beyond the Secret Service, hordes of everyday people are already choking not only the U.S. Capitol but the city itself.

"I guess we got our inaugurations mixed up" is all he can offer them.

"It ain't exactly like mixing up Ray's Famous Pizza with Famous Ray's Pizza," Pacific points out.

"And why are we here and not the others?" Lena demands.

"Tarr, I know as much as you right now, which is diddly-shit. I'm standing where the silent gentlemen with guns told me to stand."

They hear the clacking of Jett's five-inch heels before all turn to see her bounding up the steps to join them.

"Well!" she proclaims, brightly. "It's not a mistake. We're supposed to be here!"

Bronko stares down at her as if Jett has just walked out of a comic book.

"Jett, girl, I don't even know how to take in what you just said."

"That's impossible!" Lena insists.

"I'm telling you, I just spoke with the *White House event coordinator*."

Jett is practically bursting with kinetic energy, and Lena half-expects to see a rainbow form when she blows.

"They know who we are," Jett continues. "Sin du Jour, all of us, individually. They have all our names, our menu, and everything has been approved. We all have security clearance!"

"Even me?" Pacific asks, toking on a joint he somehow ninja-sparked without anyone noticing.

Bronko reaches up and quickly closes his entire fist around the hand-rolled misdemeanor, crushing it.

"Jesus Harold Chang, Pac!"

"Like I'm the first dude to get high at a presidential inauguration!" Pacific protests, causing Mr. Mirabel to laugh until he begins hacking into his oxygen tube.

Pacific pats him gently on the back until the old man recovers.

"Can we focus?" Lena interjects. "This doesn't make any sense. Did Allensworth say anything to you, Chef?"

"Not a damn word, and he went on ahead with the rest of the line and the other truck. They gotta be wonderin' where we are."

"They confiscated all our phones," Dorsky reminds him.

"That's a perfectly standard security procedure," Jett assures them all.

Lena's gaze is hot enough to melt titanium. "Jett, Jesus! I know shit like this is basically meth to you, but can you join us in reality? We're not supposed to be here!"

"Well, they're expecting us to set up and serve the VIP guests inside the Capitol immediately, and Secret Service won't let us leave. That's reality too, Lena. I would assume the *Sceadu* inauguration is proceeding as normal with the rest of the staff. I saw to all the non-food preparations for the event yesterday. The space is prepared. It's ready to go. I'm choosing to see opportunity instead of catastrophe."

Lena looks up at Bronko helplessly. "Chef, this is insane. Like, way more insane than the usual amount of insane."

"I know," he says heavily. "Something's up. Something is way off here. But there's nothing we can do about it right now except go with the flow and hope Allensworth or somebody in the know shows up and fixes this."

"So, we're serving?" Dorsky asks.

Bronko nods. "We'll plate what we got until we run out. Everything was split pretty much down the middle between the two trucks, food and equipment. We got servers. Hell, I've pulled off bigger Hollywood gigs with less; that's not the problem."

Jett applauds, ecstatic. "Excellent! I've seen the space inside. It's perfect. It doesn't even need any touches, which is good because I don't think we should let the Secret Service know there's a van full of the undead parked next to the food."

Lena just stares at her in awe. She realizes she's no longer even angry with Jett.

In fact, she's almost envious of the woman.

"Pac, you light up again in our nation's capital and I'll

beat your ass to a citrus pulp. Y'hear?"

"My bad, duder."

Jett lights up, recalling something suddenly. "Oh, and Byron! Apparently, the president-elect is a *huge* fan of yours! He always wanted to have one of your restaurants in his Atlantic City hotels."

Judging strictly by his reaction, Bronko might've just had a lit turd put out in his eye socket.

"Thank you, Jett," he says, seeing no value in correcting her perception of the matter. "That just . . . That just solidifies this moment in a way nothin' else could."

She beams back at him, wonderfully oblivious to either his tone or the look on his face.

"All right, everybody hop to," Bronko instructs. "We're short-staffed, so everybody pitch in with setup."

Dorsky, Jett, Pacific, and Mr. Mirabel begin descending the steps.

Lena lingers, stepping close to Bronko. "Chef?"

"Yeah, Tarr?"

"Forget about that racist ass-head they're inaugurating for a second," she says. "Do you think . . . is you know, the *outgoing* president here? Somewhere?"

He sighs. "I don't know, Tarr. I didn't vote for either of 'em."

TREADING WATER

"Where the heck are they?" Nikki asks no one, everyone, but mostly herself.

Rollo only shrugs. He and the rest of the kitchen line are milling about behind their rented moving truck.

Nikki tries her iPhone again, and again has no signal.

"Darren, is your phone working?" she asks, receiving no answer. "Darren?"

She looks past the small assemblage and spots Darren cloaked in shadow on the other side of the truck.

"Darren!"

"I have no reception, Nikki," James offers, helpfully, but he frowns back at the darkened spot where Darren is continuing to ignore the rest of them.

Nikki angrily stuffs her phone back inside her smock. "Well, this is awesome."

They're somewhere just across the Virginia border, lost in the still-lush forests that exist in such places. The *Sceadu* have gone all out for the inauguration of their first human president (who is actually an incubus, but apparently politicians in the supernatural world are no more honest than their human counterparts). There's a fifty-by-fifty platform of solid black onyx hovering twenty feet above the surface of a small lake. They can all see the robed, hooded figures stationed at regular intervals around the lakeshore. If you walk between them, you can actually feel the power radiating there, the magic they're using to maintain the platform's constant hovering.

Smaller slabs hover at an incline to form broad steps leading over the water from dry land. Atop the onyx surface, velvet tents of crimson and midnight blue have been erected around the perimeter. It barely needs to be lit by the ornate torches holding perfectly spherical fireballs; the onyx traps the silver rays of the moon and casts them brightly all about. In the center of the platform, a smaller dais has been raised, a stone rune serving as a podium.

Attendants are scuttling all around, servicing last-minute details before the throngs begin to arrive. Nikki and the severed half of the Sin du Jour kitchen crew watch them helplessly, at a complete loss.

"I've never known this staff to dawdle."

It's Allensworth, observing them behind his usual beatific smile. He's wearing a nondescript black tuxedo, with the exception of bloodred lapels and a matching rose pinned to the breast. His Rottweiler, Bruno, is attending Allensworth's side. The large canine rests obediently on his haunches, a red bow tie strapped around his neck in place of a collar.

"Chef Luck isn't here with our other truck, Mr. Allensworth," Nikki informs him, and immediately feels stupid for treating him like he doesn't already know everything all the time.

"Byron and the others were unexpectedly delayed on the road. They'll be along any time now. In the interim, we have a schedule to keep. I'm sure you can manage on your own to start."

"We're down half our staff and half our food!" Nikki protests.

"Miss Glowin," Allensworth begins, unruffled, "you *do*, as a professional catering company, put redundancy measures into place to prepare for unforeseen circumstances, do you not?"

Nikki sighs. "Yeah. Yes. We have extra food. We can . . . I guess we can probably manage for a couple of hours as long as there isn't a rush."

Allensworth's smile never falters. "Then please set up to begin service."

"Why can't I call anyone?" Nikki asks, holding up her phone.

"Powerful magic dampen such worldly signals," Allensworth explains, effortlessly. "And we are, as you can see, surrounded by all manner of very powerful magic."

Silently, he beckons Bruno and the two of them retreat before Nikki can question him further.

She's left cursing inside her head. Rollo, Chevet, Tenryu, and James all gather around her. Darren continues to lurk somewhere in the background.

"All right," she says resolutely a moment later. "All right. We don't have servers, so some of you are going to have to carry hors d'oeuvres."

Rollo snorts. "Why you get to tell us what to do? If Dorsky is not here, I am in charge of line."

Nikki digs her fists into her hips and her eyes become Old West gunfighter slits. "Rollo, laughing at all of Dorsky's stupid fucking jokes doesn't make you his understudy. I'm the only one with any kind of title here, and I'm the only one Chef Luck would want running things and you damn well know it. Now, does anybody else have a problem with that?"

Rollo looks around for the support of his comrades and instead finds a bunch of strangers in white smocks staring at the grass.

"Cowards," he mutters.

Nikki nods once, grunting. "Okay, then. Start setting up and then we'll get prep done."

They all disperse, even Rollo. Nikki is quick to take James by the arm, pulling him aside.

"What's wrong with him?" she asks, nodding toward

Darren, still slumped in the shadow of the truck near the tree line.

"I do not know," James quietly answers. "He will not talk to me. Since he finally began talking to me, I could not make him stop, but now . . . nothing."

"Can he work?"

James nods. "But it is like he's not even knowing he's doing it. The rest of him is . . . far away."

"Well, that'll have to do for right now. I'm sorry, James. I'll get Lena to talk to him when they finally show up."

James nods, trying to put on an optimistic expression because that's who he is.

Nikki forces herself to smile back at him, kindly, because that's who she is.

OFF THE RACK

Plating soup trios for hundreds of people is almost enough to make Lena forget they're in Washington, D.C., catering the *actual*, real presidential inauguration. It's enough to keep her from thinking about why the rest of the Sin du Jour crew hasn't arrived, or why they haven't been evacuated, or why they were diverted here in the first place.

It is not, however, enough to distract her from the tumbling feeling of dread stretching endlessly from the pit of her stomach.

The kitchen in the U.S. Capitol they've been given for prep and cooking is a utilitarian palace of immaculate brass fixtures and appliances. Lena could live here happily forever. A trio of ramekins sits on a single plate beside her stove. She ladles chili pork verde into one, clam chowder with bacon into the second, and a spicy miso pork ramen into the third.

She carries four plates of the three-way pork soups over to the large marble island they're using as their expediting station and finds it's already covered edge to edge in identical plates.

"I got no more room over here!" Lena yells back at Dorsky. "Why isn't this shit going out?"

"I gave the stoner five minutes to dump his ass and it's been almost fifteen."

"Dammit, Pac," Lena mutters.

Mr. Mirabel, a more portable oxygen machine slung in a leather satchel from his shoulder to keep his hands free, wheezes his way back to the island and grabs several more plates. It allows Lena to offload what she's carrying.

She turns and almost slams into Dorsky, who reaches up and gently takes her by the biceps to stabilize her.

"I'll run," he says. "You go find Pacific and drag him the hell back here."

Lena looks down at his hands, the way he's holding her and their proximity taking her back to that closet where they first hooked up, while they were hiding from their coworkers who'd been transformed into crazed sex lizards.

It shouldn't be an erotic memory, and yet.

Lena nods, slipping free of his grip deftly. "Yes, Chef," she says without irony.

She jogs out of the kitchen and finds the nearest set of bathrooms, checking both without hesitation or shame. She finds each one empty, much to her exasperation.

Rather than returning to her station, Lena decides to search the nearest rooms beyond the facilities. She finds several locked doors and open rooms with the lights out. Anyone that takes notice of her seems to only need to spy the logo on the breast of her smock to dismiss any further interest. Lena supposes if she's been given clearance to know secrets about the world forbidden to 99 percent of the population, she's got clearance to wander around the U.S. Capitol.

Lena is ready to give up and is literally turning around to walk back to the kitchen when he skirts past her. It's not Pacific. It is possibly the farthest thing from Pacific she could conjure to mind.

Lena recognizes the man instantly and on sight, of course. There's no mistaking that red face or the hideous hay-colored rat's nest of a rug she's always wondered if he wears ironically.

An immediate, empty loathing fills her stomach and a more active, seething hate bubbles atop her brain.

The newly elected president of the United States brushes by without even seeming to notice her. He strides down the hall, unencumbered and unescorted, which Lena immediately finds odd.

She's following him before she realizes she's doing it, and once she becomes fully aware, somehow Lena can't stop. She maintains a comfortable distance, but he still seems completely oblivious to his surroundings anyway.

Lena asks herself what she's doing and no answer is

forthcoming. Is she going to assassinate the asshole? Somehow, it seems perfectly plausible as long as she doesn't think through it thoroughly. That's one of the problems with working at Sin du Jour: everything you experience starts to make you believe anything is possible, but that "anything" is rarely a good thing.

Usually, that impossible thing is hideous.

She watches the soon-to-be president enter a room with its double glass doors pulled open. The space beyond is brightly lit. Lena knows she should turn back now, but it all seems too easy, too weird and rare and inviting to stop now.

She follows him inside.

The half of the room she can see is empty. Tall black curtains partition off the other half of the room. Two attendants, hulking men in steel-gray tunics with buttons the size of silver dollars, are stationed where the folds of the curtain meet.

As she looks on, the president-elect removes his suit jacket and hands it off to an attendant. He then flips his tie over one shoulder and proceeds to unbutton the four middle buttons of his dress shirt. Lena thinks he's going to keep undressing, but instead he just stands there, silent and still. Then, a moment or two later, his back arches sharply in one jerking motion. His arms are thrown back, and his eyes go wide and dead.

Lena feels her every muscle tense as she watches something begin to push its way through the open fold in the president-elect's shirt. She squints, wanting to close her eyes, every horrific thing she's witnessed since coming to work for Sin du Jour flashing through her mind all at once.

The thing forces its way out of the president-elect's body, through his unbuttoned shirt, and unfurls down his body.

Lena prepares to look away, jaw clenched, but she stops.

It's a ladder.

It's a tiny rope ladder.

Lena is now squinting in confusion rather than horror or terror. There is simply no denying the fact that a miniature rope ladder has been deployed from inside the president-elect's shirt, and is now hanging down to his knees.

It's somehow far less shocking when the little green creature crawls out through the president-elect's shirt and begins descending the ladder, making a noise that sounds to Lena like an old man forced to traverse a flight of stairs. As its clawed hands and feet grip each wooden rung, Lena notices the rungs have been carved with crude designs and slogans in English. They remind her of pictures she's seen of the way soldiers decorated the stocks of their shotguns in trenches during the First World War.

The creature is two to three feet tall, bipedal, and has the face of a French bulldog without the charm or humanity. Its skin is dry and cracked, and its color has the dusty, faded appearance of once-vibrant paint long dried. It leaps from the last rung of the ladder and hits the ground with a triumphant hoot.

The attendants bow respectfully to the creature, then they each take a fold of the dark curtain partition and begin peeling them back to open up the rest of the room.

In the next moment, Lena finds she's relocated her sense of horror.

In fact, it's far deeper and much, much worse than it was just a few seconds ago.

As the creature pads casually away, the attendants pick up the president-elect shell it was wearing and carry it over to a dangling cradle. The cradle is hanging from what resembles a large dry-cleaning rack. The rack is filled with them, their leather shoes swinging a foot above the ground.

It's an entire rack of ghastly realistic human puppets.

There are several copies of the president-elect. There is an equal number of his primary opponent. They're surrounded by what must be every recognizable politician Lena has ever glimpsed on CNN. There are hundreds of them, slabs of meat on hooks, wearing designer suits and staring at the ceiling with inanimate eyes.

A rising chorus of nasal chattering begins to register in Lena's ears, and her instinct to follow the sound to its source is probably all that keeps her from turning and running away. To the far left of the human-puppet rack, a dozen of those same creatures are crowded around a folding table. They're drinking mugs of coffee and snacking on frosted pastries. The entire tableau is engulfed in a cloud of thin, wispy, herbal smoke.

And they're not alone.

"Pac?" Lena asks, and shock doesn't even begin to cover it.

This is like waking up inside a surrealist's painting.

"What up, Lena?" Pacific greets her warmly as he passes one of his joints to the nearest green-skinned puppet operator.

The creature clips it between the ends of two claws and tokes expertly.

"What the fu—"

"You never quite get used to it, do you?" an instantly recognizable baritone voice asks.

Lena spins around, and what she sees is almost as shocking as the scene she's left behind.

He's a full head taller than her, and up close, the lines in his face run deeper and the stark gray consuming his hair appears more ancient than in any picture.

Everyone's always talking about how eight short years in the White House aged him fifty years.

They're righter than they know.

It's him.

It's the outgoing president of the United States.

"I uh, apologize," he says. "I didn't mean to startle you."

You almost said "fuck" in front of the president, her brain remarks.

"No," Lena manages. "No, it's fine. Totally fine. I just got . . . lost."

"You're the caterer, yes?"

"I . . . um . . . one of them, yeah. Yes."

He laughs. "I, uh . . . I really enjoyed the all-pork theme to the menu tonight. I'm not, uh, sure a lot of folks here . . . you know . . . got the joke, as such, but the First Lady and I really got a kick out of it, let me tell you."

"Oh, thank you. That . . . I . . . It was actually my idea." Her brain sends a signal that is the equivalent of someone kicking you underneath a table, and she adds, "Mr. President. Sir."

He lowers his voice, as if confiding in her solely. "It's not exactly a, uh, pleasant occasion for a lot of us. What with . . ."

He waves his hand toward the lifeless, dangling husks of the president-elect on the rack.

" . . . *that,*" he continues, "being sworn in tonight. So I, uh, genuinely do appreciate the levity you all brought. It was needed."

"Sir, what . . . What is . . . What are . . ."

Lena tries to mimic his wave, indicating the entire rack behind her.

He stares down at her in brief puzzlement. "Oh, you must be, uh, new to the company, then? Catering these types of events?"

Lena just nods dumbly.

"Well, individual, sentient candidates went 'out of style,' as it were, quite a long time ago. It seemed redundant, I suppose. Since, as I'm sure you *do* know, there's no real difference, on a practical level, between either major party. The *Sceadu* sets most of our overriding policies and legislates all watershed-type matters. What we do is largely for the masses, not that we don't try to make changes where and when we can. But to avoid personality clashes or any one candidate 'rocking the boat,' they started running what we call on the Hill 'meat puppets.'"

"Okay. And what are they?" Lena asks, pointing at the creatures getting high with her busboy.

"Oh, them? Gremlins!" the president proclaims, a genuine affection underlying the power in his voice.

"Like . . . Gizmo?"

He laughs again. "No, no. Uh . . . gremlins are actually some of our nation's oldest civil servants. Dating as far back as the Revolutionary War. They sabotaged ships of the British Royal Navy in aid of the Continental forces. During World War One and Two, elite gremlin squads were actually responsible for the destruction of more enemy fighters and bomber planes than our own pilots. Highly patriotic, gremlins. Highly."

"So they . . . they, like, operate . . . the meat puppets?"

"They're good at taking direction, but also improvising within parameters, actually. They tried to break into Hollywood at one point, but the goblins squashed that right away. You know, I, uh . . . I actually hear it took three gremlins just to operate President Taft?" He laughs then, loudly, genuinely amused by the thought. "He was, uh . . . he was a large man, to be sure."

"But wait, you're not . . . ?" Lena asks, trailing off, unable to even consciously choose the right words.

"A meat puppet? Oh, no. No. I am . . . or was . . . the first human candidate to take the White House in over a hundred years, I believe. You think the, uh, you think the American people were surprised I won? Well, let me tell you . . ."

He laughs, long and jovially at the memories obviously flooding his mind's eye in that moment.

"Okay," Lena says. "All right. But I mean . . . what do you . . . like, what do you actually do, then? Or what did you do? As president?"

He sighs. "I mean . . . you do what you can, right? Most of the, uh, the big decisions are influenced or outright decided by the various factions comprising the *Sceadu*. They're so deeply interwoven through politics and private industry. I tried to help humans, American humans, in ways that didn't threaten the *Sceadu*. Was, I uh, overly optimistic? Probably. Probably. But I tried. I purely did try. And there's a lot of which I'll leave this office proud."

Listening as he speaks, sharing thoughts so private and personal, has the exact opposite effect on Lena she might've otherwise expected. That deep sense of dread returns, the feeling that's been spiraling down into the pit of her stomach since she first saw the freeway signs for Washington, D.C. If anything, that feeling is even more pronounced now, more impending and terrifyingly real.

"Sir, may I ask you kind of a personal question?"

"Please," he encourages her without hesitation.

"What about all that shi—" She pauses. "Uh, all that stuff you don't think you can change? What do you do when you feel . . . I don't know, like a train barreling down and everything is bolted to the tracks in front of it and all you can do is watch, knowing what's about to happen?"

The president takes a deep, contemplative breath, sliding his hands into his pockets, as he seems to very seriously consider the question.

"I would say . . . at that point, you make a choice. And

in aid of that choice, you ask yourself a question. 'Is it worth it?' That's the only question that matters, really. If it isn't worth it, if it's not the hill on which you're meant to die, you choose to let it go and deal with the fallout. If it *is* worth it . . ."

Lena waits, his answer seeming in that moment to mean more to her than any answer to any question she's ever asked.

"Yes?" she presses.

"Then, I suppose, you have to hope against all reason that your body is enough to stop that train."

It takes time for that to fully settle with her, but when it does, a calm overtakes Lena.

"Thank you, sir," she says. Then, turning around and yelling to Pacific: "Pac! Get your ass back to the kitchen! Now!"

"Yeah, boss! On my way!"

Lena very politely excuses herself and runs full-speed back to the kitchen.

She finds Bronko puzzling over plastic bins filled Nikki's churro chicharrónes.

"I don't recall exactly how Nikki wanted to finish these—" he begins, but Lena cuts him off.

"Chef, we have to get out of here. Now."

He looks up at her, expression turning from business to grave. "How's that, now?"

"Something terrible is going to happen at the *Sceadu* inauguration. I know it. We have to get out of here and try to stop it. We *have* to."

TRAIN TO CATCH

"What time do they inaugurate Consoné?" Lena asks Bronko.

"Midnight. That's the tradition."

They're bussing after dessert service, as the VIP guests all file out of the banquet hall to join the spectators on the steps and colonnades outside of the Capitol Building. They'll be swearing in the new president of the United States soon. They've heard gossip the crowd gathered beyond the security perimeter is record-breaking and terrifyingly partisan, an organic bomb waiting for a spark.

"Then we can still make it if we leave now," Lena insists.

"We all know you're good with a paring knife," Dorsky tells her, "but you ain't John Wick. The Secret Service won't let us leave. There're a lot more of them and they all have guns."

Lena is resolved. "If we can just get to that crowd out front, we can ditch our smocks and mix in. There's no way they'll be able to spot us."

"It's fucking government security, Lena!" Dorsky explodes. "They see everything!"

"Oh, bullshit!" she fires back at him. "This is all bullshit, Tag. It's an illusion. It's meat puppets on parade. It's *literally* run by fucking meat puppets. Everything everyone thinks about this place and these people is a lie. There's no power here. You want to know who I think the most important people are in Washington tonight? Seriously? Us. Because Allensworth wants us to be trapped here, and he and people . . . and *things* like him, they're the ones who actually see everything. This, all of this, is a fucking shadowbox."

Her words are enough to shut down Dorsky, but Bronko is quick to ask, "Don't that amount to the same thing? If Allensworth wants us here, isn't it him we're trying to sneak past?"

Lena shakes her head. "He isn't here. He's where the real power is, in some backwoods in rural fucking Virginia right now. I'm betting he expects us to be exactly what I was when we pulled in here tonight: overwhelmed and scared and falling in line out of habit."

"Why are you so damn sure something that bad is up, Tarr?" Bronko asks her. "And what do you imagine is about to happen?"

Lena hasn't articulated it fully for herself yet, perhaps because she doesn't really want to.

"It's all about Consoné," she says. "Allensworth wanted to take him down, and he was willing to wipe out hundreds of humans and goblins to do it. That didn't work. We screwed it up and Consoné won. Allensworth has to take out Consoné directly now. And the only reason he hasn't made us pay for our part in ruining his plans is because we're still valuable. We're still the cooks. We're the invisible servants they let go anywhere and get near anyone."

"What are you saying?" Dorsky asked, genuinely lost.

Bronko, however, looks as though he's catching up.

"Darren," she says, darkly.

Bronko nods.

"Boy's been . . . way off lately," he admits.

"It's more than that," she insists. "I didn't want to see it. I didn't want to call him on it, out of guilt. But he's not himself. It has to be him. Allensworth is using him to do something horrible. Tonight. I know it."

"All right, then," Bronko says, the same resolve that's overtaken Lena seeming to have infected him. "How do we get to the crowd, past the revenue men?"

"A distraction," Lena says. "It needs to be a big one. Pac, would your new gremlin pals help out?"

Pacific shakes his head. "Those dudes are serious about serving their country, man. They'd *never* go against the office. They're pretty socially liberal, which is nice."

"Pretty damn easy to cause a ruckus at an event where the president is speaking, seems to me," Bronko says. "Especially this one. Somebody's just gotta go after him."

Lena nods. "The only problem with that is whoever makes the play isn't leaving with us."

Bronko says, "I just said it was the easiest way to cause a ruckus."

"Normally, I'd volunteer, y'all," Pacific chimes in, "but I'm not sure I have the motor coordination at this point in the evening, y'know?"

"I'll do it," Dorsky says.

Bronko and Lena both stare silently at him in collective shock.

"Don't normally know you to change your mind so fast, Tag," Bronko says.

Dorsky looks at Lena. "It needs to be done, right? We're running out of time, right? I'll do it. Hopefully, they won't shoot me."

"Nah, you're the wrong complexion for that," Pacific points out.

"Don't do this for me," Lena practically scolds him. "If that's what this is. Don't do it because—"

"You convinced me, all right? If Allensworth is coming after my line, then this is what I'm prepared to do. Let's do it. Now."

Bronko reaches up and grips his shoulder, claps him on the back. "Don't worry; they won't kill ya. And if we have to, Ritter and the team'll bust you right out of whatever black-box prison they send you to."

"That's really comforting, Chef, thanks."

They deposit the remnants of dessert and coffee and what's left of cocktail glasses in the kitchen, then the five of them head outside. Oddly, it's not the Secret Service or White House staff that gives them any flack; it's the producers running the setup to broadcast the inauguration nationally.

They find themselves ushered and massed directly to the right of the inaugural podium. The shortest path to the barricades holding back the public is a fifty-yard dash down the stone steps below. There's police and Secret Service staffing those barricades every few feet, however. All Lena and the rest can do is wait.

It would be thoroughly boring if it weren't for the knowledge of what they're about to attempt mainlining adrenaline and anticipation throughout their bodies. Lena watches the chief justice take his position near the podium, holding the book with which he'll swear in the new president. Lena can't make out what the book is, but knowing the candidate's image, she assumes it's a copy of the *Necronomicon*.

Half an hour passes. They hear the crowd before they

see him, half of them exulting like it's Nuremberg circa 1938, the other half ready to crucify like they're in the gallery of the war crime tribunals held there later. The president-elect walks out in his formal winter best to meet the chief justice and to be sworn in as president of the United States.

Lena looks up at their faces: Bronko and Dorsky, Pacific and Mo. They're all still looking at him like he's human instead of a meat puppet being piloted by an overly patriotic gremlin.

"I liked his show, you know," Dorsky remarks, nervously. "'You're fired.' All that. It was funny. It was a funny show."

"Are you okay?" Lena asks.

"Fuck, no, I'm not okay," he spits back at her, annoyed. "This is all insane, everything that's happening, this whole world. It's fucking off its tit."

"Glad you're finally getting that."

"I just wanted to cook."

"I know."

"I just wanted to run my own kitchen."

"I know, Tag."

"I can deal with goblins and demons and trolls and all of that shit, but this—"

"Tag, listen to me," Lena says, gripping his wrist. "You don't *have* to do this. We can think of something—"

Before she can say the next word, his wrist has left her hand and Lena realizes he's leapt out onto the inauguration platform. Dorsky breaks into a run, using his longest stride, becoming a missile aimed at that podium in the center.

He doesn't make it four feet before three Secret Service agents tackle him to the ground.

It's over in a split second and about as anticlimactic as a climax can be. In fact, it has the exact opposite effect of distracting the crowd. The first several yards of the surrounding throng falls deafly silent except for brief gasps and a scattered exclamation. No one else moves. The entire scene freezes as if it's the final scene of a 1980s sitcom episode. It's like a spotlight made of a hundred thousand eyes has been shone right in front of them.

"Shit on us," Bronko mutters.

Lena's heart sinks a foot below her chest and her brain burns with frustration and panic.

It's still quiet enough for a gentle scraping sound to draw Lena's attention away from Dorsky being subdued on the concrete four feet away. What she sees when she locates the source of the noise wipes away all of those feelings and sensations, replacing them with abject surprise.

It wasn't a large enough distraction to cover the four of

them breaking into a run down the U.S. Capitol steps.

It was, however, enough of a distraction that no one seems to notice or process the slender oxygen canister rolling across the plateau toward the podium.

Even those who see it can't or don't fully comprehend the ramifications of the lit bundle of matches perched precariously where a tube should be connected to the canister. The metal cylinder rolls directly toward the president-elect, stopping when it hits the polished toes of his wing tips.

Lena glances frantically back at Mr. Mirabel. The air tube perpetually attached to his nostrils is still there, but he's slowly twirling the opposite, detached end like a lasso.

He shrugs at her.

Lena looks back just in time to see the oxygen canister explode at the meat puppet's feet in a tornado of white. There's no blood. There's no gore. There are only patches of fabric and chunks of what looks like flesh-colored tofu flying through the night. The storm of dry meat chunks rains down and splats against the plateau around the podium, creating a sickly mound of half-melted reddish pink.

That's not the worst part.

They hear the first faraway sounds of the shrieking a moment after the meat-puppet chunks settle. The shriek grows louder and louder until a small green blur reappears in the hot stage lights erected for the television cameras. The gremlin lands directly in the middle of the meat-puppet puddle, the concrete-softened, half-liquefied stuffing helping to break its fall. The gremlin rights itself, dazed, and begins wildly shaking off the reddish pink goo, throwing it everywhere and on everyone nearby like a shaggy dog out of the bath.

It stops, staring out at the crowd from the middle of what used to be the most controversial president-elect in the history of America.

That's when everyone finally loses his or her shit.

It's the screaming, frothing chaos Lena was hoping for when Dorsky made his move. Secret Service rush the podium. Politicians and celebrities flee. Most importantly, the barricades holding back the public are overrun in less than sixty seconds. Police, protestors, supporters, and everyone in between are embroiled in all-out, mass-psychosis-driven warfare.

"Let's go!" Bronko shouts over the madness.

"Mo can't make it without his tank!" Pacific yells. "I'll chill here with him. You guys handle business!"

There's no time to argue. Bronko and Lena begin pushing their way down the steps, trying to keep tightly together as they go.

"Stop right there!"

Two Secret Service agents with pistols drawn, spaced far enough apart to be a problem, and everyone is giving their firearms a wide berth.

Lena and Bronko are stuck.

"Gentlemen! Gentlemen! I'm afraid I'm going to have to order you to lower those weapons and let these folks pass!"

Lena turns her head and looks past Bronko, recognizing that voice instantly just as she did standing in front of the meat-puppet rack.

The outgoing president, long winter coat whipping about him and gloved hand raised like an image from a comic book cover, is commanding the Secret Service to stand down.

"Sir, you should step back—" one of the agents begins.

"Son, I'd like to think I still brook some authority around here. Now, these people are on business vital to our nation's security, and I *insist* you let them pass."

Lena looks to Bronko, who she's certain she could knock over in that moment by poking him in the chest, then back at the Secret Service agents.

They slowly lower their weapons.

Lena slaps Bronko on the arm to snap him out of his disbelief.

"Thank you again, sir!" she shouts to the president.

As they break into a run between the agents, heading into the thick of the crowd, Lena hears him yell after them both: "Good luck with that train!"

SECRET WEAPON

In the tent given to Sin du Jour to prep their *Sceadu* presidential inauguration fare, Nikki is drizzling chipotle-and-Kahlúa chocolate sauce over small paper-lined baskets of churro chicharrónes. Designing a dessert for an all-pork menu, let alone a formal all-pork menu, wasn't easy, and Nikki isn't a particular fan of fried pastries to begin with, but she pushed herself as she always does and is pretty damn pleased with the results.

James pops his head in, sweat dappling his bald scalp. "The ones that are part horse have eaten all that we brought for them."

The rest of the line refers to centaurs and minotaurs as "half-and-half," a term Jett constantly reminds them is pejorative. Nikki knows James is just doing the best with the English he's learned over the past several years after arriving in New York City from Senegal.

"Then they're going to have to eat what everyone else is eating," she says impatiently.

He nods, backing away from the tent flaps.

"And I need arms to serve dessert!" Nikki yells after him.

"I will try, but everyone is in the weeds. I cannot find Darren."

That stops Nikki cold. "You can't . . . what? You can't *find* Darren?"

"No, Chef."

Nikki explodes. "I cannot *believe* . . ." Then a thought seems to occur to her, breaking through that burst of anger. "Oh, thank you for calling me 'Chef'. That is so sweet of you, James; I love you." Nikki shakes her head as if shaking the burst of levity away. "But no! No, that is some BS right there!"

Despite finding herself suddenly in charge of the entire event, or perhaps because of having that responsibility thrust upon her, Nikki can't stop herself. She leaves the tent and strides through the party space, around the currently unoccupied inaugural dais. She weaves through the guests in her soiled chef's smock, ignoring the several celebrity faces of goblins she registers.

She passes by Allensworth, who raises a glass of champagne to her with that perpetual smile that only mocks genuine human emotion.

Nikki ignores him.

She exits the hovering platform, jogging down the suspended steps of onyx and leaping over the final one onto the shore of the lake. She walks toward the tree line, leaving the straggling party guests and the cacophony of the crowd behind.

Nikki approaches the back of Sin du Jour's rented truck, finding it half-open and unattended.

"Darren! Are you out here? What the heck is up, man? You're leaving the rest of us in the weeds!"

There's no answer, but her eyes catch a glint, a strip of light cast from inside the truck.

"Darren? Seriously, dude!"

Nikki marches over to the back of the truck and climbs up over the edge of the loading door.

"Darren!"

Hoisting herself up to her feet with great effort, Nikki's eyes have to adjust to the darkness filling the back of the large space, but her ears are assaulted with both the sound of cutting air and a feral growling punctuated with occasional shrieking battle cries.

Darren is stripped to the waist. He's armed with a six-foot spear ending in a sword-length blade. The other end is crowned with a jewel that gleams all at once blue, red, and green in the dark. Darren is twirling the shaft and slashing with the blade like a master in a kung fu movie.

"Darren?"

He stops in mid-stroke, halting with his back to her. He stands perfectly still and straight except for the slight motion of his shoulders moving in time with his labored breath.

"What are you doing?" she asks.

"It's almost time," he says in a voice that sounds nothing like Darren's, especially with his back turned to her like that.

"Time . . . for what?"

"You shouldn't be here."

Everything in Nikki's body, everything she's spent a lifetime accruing as a woman who walks alone in the streets every day and night, is now telling her to run.

"Yeah . . . yeah, I get that sense. I'll just go, okay? I'll go get James. Maybe we can all talk about—"

"You can't go."

"I'm happy to stay if it's so we can talk about what's going on with you. But you'd need to put that weird-ass spear down. Where were you hiding that thing, anyway?"

Almost before she's done asking the question, the blade retracts into the shaft of the spear and its entire length folds impossibly inward until it becomes a single, foot-long haft.

"Oh," Nikki manages around the lump in her throat.

"You can't go," Darren repeats in his alien voice.

"I'm not going anywhere," Nikki assures him, after which she immediately turns to bolt from the back of the truck.

She never feels the jewel end of the spear collide with the back of her skull. Nikki is only aware of the thick veil of darkness that drips over her vision like molasses, and the curious sensation of ordering her limbs to move and her limbs not obeying.

She does feel the floor of the truck rush up and smack the shit out of her, however.

Then she's out.

THY LIFE BE MINE
TO TAKE OR SAVE

Nikki watches Darren roll a black undershirt over an abdomen that looks as though it was drawn for the cover of an erotic novel.

It only confirms a theory she's long held: having six-pack abs makes you evil.

Her wrists are tied together with bungee cord around a large metal rivet in the truck's trailer wall. Her ankles have been similarly bound, and Darren used a linen napkin to gag her. He hasn't harmed her beyond knocking her unconscious, but the dull throbbing in the back of her skull and the way the entire world is thrown off its axis when she moves her chin is harm enough for her liking.

"The nexus ascends soon," he says to himself, almost like a mantra or a monk's chant. "The nexus wearing a king's flesh. That flesh must be torn asunder if the ascension is to invert into oblivion. Shed the man-cloak, annihilate the nexus."

It sounds like gibberish until she latches on to the

words "king" and "ascension." They revolve around each other in her mind until they raise images there. Nikki's eyes widen. She realizes whom he's talking about, for whom that spear is meant.

Consoné.

Darren pulls on his white Sin du Jour chef's smock and begins slowly and methodically buttoning it.

Nikki shouts garbled sentences at him through her gag.

His fingers never waver from their task.

She begins thrashing her body against the floor and wall of the trailer.

That gets his attention.

Darren strides across the trailer floor and grabs her by the hair, painfully, destroying one of her victory rolls and sending hairpins flying like shrapnel as he jerks her head to one side.

Nikki ceases thrashing, but she stares defiantly up into his eyes and begins calmly speaking through the gag, despite the fact her words don't come across any clearer.

He's watching her the way a burgeoning psychopath, when they're young, watches bugs crawl among the shrubs. There's no humanity in those eyes, and nothing of the kind, shy boy she met alongside Lena so many months ago.

With his free hand, Darren reaches up and carefully removes the wadded linen from her mouth.

Nikki launches into a rapid-fire litany without even drawing a fresh breath.

"Look, Darren, we're all really proud of you getting in shape and doing martial arts and gaining self-confidence and your beard looks great, but assassinating the president of the secret supernatural government that controls, like, everything is *not cool*, dude!"

"There is no king," he answers, mechanically. "There is only a flesh nexus. I have seen what converges there, within it. I have seen myself on the other side of a shattered mirror. The nexus must be destroyed."

"Is that . . . like, from *True Detective*? The Matthew McConaughey one, before it was shitty?"

"When the nexus collapses, the other side of the mirror becomes void," he assures her, or perhaps himself. "Nothingness. No eyes stare back. I will be all that remains, singular and purified."

"Darren . . . someone or something has messed around with your mind, and whatever you think doing this is going to accomplish, it won't."

"I am all that will remain—"

"Did Ritter teach you this?" Nikki asks over his ravings.

The question gives Darren pause. He stares through her, his eyes seeming to search, and in the sparse light she's certain she sees his jaw tremble.

"Darren, Ritter wouldn't want you to do this," she presses. "This isn't what he's been teaching you—"

He stuffs the linen napkin back inside her mouth, roughly this time. His jaw tightens, and Darren's eyes that contain nothing of their owner's self refocus on her intently.

"There will be no ascension," he reaffirms.

Nikki thrashes anew and yells through the gag, but it's clear he's done listening to her. Darren walks across the trailer floor and picks up the jeweled spear folded into its nondescript foot-long form. He slips the cylinder inside the cuff of his left smock sleeve, concealing it easily there.

Darren takes a moment to straighten his collar and tug the hem of his smock. He smooths his close-cropped hair and runs his fingers through his beard.

To anyone who doesn't know him intimately, he looks perfectly normal and forgettable.

No one at the inauguration will so much as stop to question him.

Darren walks to the front of the trailer and raises the door just enough to slip under. Nikki takes the opportunity to create as much noise as possible but stops when the door slams home and she realizes she's sitting alone in the dark inside a truck parked in the middle of the woods.

Nikki tries a few times to tug apart her wrists and ankles but inevitably gives that up as futile, too.

Leaning her damaged skull carefully against the wall of the trailer, she wonders idly and inexplicably if the guests are enjoying her drizzled churro chicharrónes.

THE TRAIN, THE TRACKS, THE PENNY

It's ten to midnight.

Tradition dictates that its newly elected president receives the blessing of a representative of each founding race of the *Sceadu* (of course, that's in the modern parlance; a thousand years ago, tradition would've dictated the newly anointed Bardic Ovate Archdruid participate in a ritual orgy with offerings from each race). On the dais in the center of the hovering onyx platform, those *Sceadu* race representatives take their place in the formal reception line.

Several dozen gnomes have linked up in their piecemeal disguises to form a single slight Japanese businessman to represent the elementals. An elegant, middle-aged woman draped in sheer silk has been dispatched by the witch covens. The Goblin King has sent one of the stars, the beefcake one, from one of those awful superhero franchises. A graying minotaur stands for the taurian races. Finally, Allensworth waits to give the blessing of humankind.

Conspicuous by their absence from the dais is any demon clan elder. There isn't a single demon in attendance at the inauguration, in fact. Even the youngest and most Earthly integrated of the demon clans, the suit-clad Vig'nerash, have failed to attend. It's a silent but strong form of protest over the election of what they perceive as a human to the highest office in the earthbound supernatural world.

"Ladies, gentlemen, extrahumans of all stripes," Allensworth addresses the crowd. "We gather tonight to receive the next in a long line of venerable leaders of the oldest and most venerable organization on this mortal plane. They've been warriors, great thinkers, great magicians, and occasionally all three."

Allensworth gives pause for the scattered laughter.

"Tonight, for the first time, the *Sceadu* receives a human at the head of its table. An extraordinary human, to be sure."

If there was sarcasm in his voice, a machine programmed to recognize such tones wouldn't mark it.

"Welcome with me now the new president of the Sceadu, Enzo Consoné!"

Allensworth begins the next round of applause, stepping back into the receiving line.

Enzo Consoné is resplendent in his finest black pinstriped Italian suit. A full-length alligator-skin coat dyed jet to match is draped over his broad shoulders.

Consoné's hulking satyr bodyguard, Claudius, keeps close pace with his charge. He's also decked out in fine Italian sartorial splendor, tailored to perfectly hide his goatlike hindquarters and hooves.

The duo ascends the dais to warm, jovial applause and cheers. Consoné acknowledges the reception and the assemblage gratefully, waving, making direct eye contract with as many attendees as possible.

He raises his hands to silence the approbation. "Thank you! Thank you, my friends!

"For time untold, the *Sceadu* has served to protect the peace and covenant of our respective societies. As the world has changed around us, we've preserved the secrets of that covenant and the existence of our brothers and sisters from those who would do them harm. Many of whom, I realize, look like me. But that's the point. That's why I sought the presidency of the *Sceadu*. It's time for a new era of understanding, of integration, of cooperation. It's time for the *Sceadu* ... to emerge from the shadow."

Those who've come to celebrate his inauguration thrill and practically combust at Enzo Consoné's words, each sentence feeding their deepest desires. While some fear his ideas mean losing themselves to a human world, others choose to believe he'll elevate them to a new status.

Everyone with hands to do so applauds, except Allensworth.

Amid the celebration, no one takes notice of the handsome, bearded young server kneeling with his tray of champagne flutes in front of the dais. If anyone does, they surely think he dropped something or must be tying his shoe.

"Hold the hell on, girl!" Bronko calls to Lena from the bottom of the floating onyx steps.

She's already reached the platform by the time he's taking the first one.

"Hurry up, Chef!" she calls back.

The entire crowd is mustered in front of her, between the dais and the steps. A quick scan reveals nothing to Lena but a single mass of flesh whose prominent feature is the back of heads. She looks above the guests to the dais itself, seeing Consoné moving gracefully and gratefully through the reception line.

She breathes a brief yet deep sigh of relief.

"There's still time, Chef," she says to Bronko as he finally joins her, huffing and puffing from the pace.

"Find Vargas" is all he says.

"Right. I've got the crowd. Check the tents and get the others."

He nods, gripping her shoulders for a moment, then strides off toward the crimson tents lining the perimeter of the platform.

Lena weaves into the back of the crowd and begins forcing her way through it, checking faces as she goes. No one registers, and there's not a single white Sin du Jour smock among them that she can spot. Lena keeps glancing back up at the dais, monitoring Consoné. Everything seems to progressing just as it should, and she begins to wonder if it's only her perception tinting the reality of the situation.

Then she reaches the front of the crowd and sees a tray filled with champagne flutes sitting on the onyx floor.

"Dammit," she hisses.

"Tarr!"

She turns to see Bronko approaching her with James in tow.

"Rest of the crew is accounted for except for Nikki and Vargas," Bronko tells her.

"I have not seen Darren in hours and Nikki disappeared before she finished plating dessert," James says.

"Nikki—" Lena begins, but before she can complete the thought, a deep, baritone scream pierces the air.

They all turn to have a severed pair of goat's legs wearing strips of fine Italian wool hit them in their smocks, smearing and splashing all three with blood.

Claudius' anguished face appears over the edge of the dais, blood dripping from his lips. He's trying desperately to pull his prone body away from something.

That something is Darren, standing where Claudius was only a moment before, holding his fully extended spear.

"Darren!" Lena yells up at him.

He doesn't appear to even register her voice. He moves so fast, his feet barely touch the top of the dais. A powerful slash of the spear shatters the Japanese businessman, sending the gnomes composing his form flying perilously in all directions. Darren spins, twirling the spear expertly, and another slash cuts the podium in half. The reception line disperses, its members backing away or outright fleeing the stage, leaving Consoné exposed and alone.

Lena looks to the sides of the dais and sees what has to be security—Allensworth's men as well as more robed figures—rushing toward it. She's torn between wanting to protect Darren and hoping madly they can save Consoné's life.

Atop the dais, Darren also sees them approaching. He twirls the spear again, holding it high and vertically with the jeweled end pointed toward the ground. As the first of the security detail ascends the dais, Darren stabs the spear downward with a deep, guttural cry.

The multicolored jewel shatters on impact, but from its core a rippling three-foot shockwave is born that lashes out in all directions simultaneously.

"Look out!" Lena hears Bronko yell right before his large form is obscuring her vision of the dais.

In the next moment, she's lying on the floor beside James. Bronko is sprawled motionless on top of them. She can barely breathe under his bulk, and all that solid mass feels as though it's crushing her bones. Lena wriggles free from beneath him, suppressing the panic and fear as if she were once again riding shotgun in an Army caravan on an IED-rich Afghan road. She crawls up to her knees.

Even a quick glance around tells her everyone who was hit by that magical shockwave is down. A more detailed glance tells her that appears to be everyone but her. They're all lying motionless. Lena, the panic bubbling up to a dangerous level, quickly leans down against Bronko's broad chest and listens for his heartbeat.

It's there. He's breathing but temporarily (at least she hopes) paralyzed.

Lena hears a voice she doesn't recognize proclaim, "The nexus contracts in the face of a new star rising!"

Darren.

She jumps to her feet and charges at the dais, leaping onto its edge as it were an obstacle back at boot. She grips the edge and hoists herself up onto its surface, staying low on one knee as she surveys the scene.

Darren is advancing on Consoné's rag-doll form, bladed end of the spear he's holding guiding the way.

"You were the one on the other side of the mirror," he says to new *Sceadu* president in that voice Lena doesn't know, despite their being best friends for over ten years. "It was always you."

"Darren, stop!" she yells, springing to her feet and practically sliding across the dais to put herself between Consoné and that spear blade.

"Stop it, Darren!" she repeats, holding up her hands. "This isn't you! Look at me, man! It's Lena! I'm your best bro—"

Darren reverses his grip on the spear without a word and strikes Lena across the jaw with the blunted end. Shards of broken jewel still attached there slash open her cheek as the force of the blow knocks her off her feet. She hits the top of the dais hard, the impact finishing the job the spear end started and sending her careening into unconsciousness.

Darren never even seemed to look at her.

He upends the spear again, pointing the tip of the blade at Consoné.

"The nexus implodes upon itself as a false star," he all but exults, raising his arms above his head and readying to strike down with the spear.

Surprisingly powerful arms seize him in a full nelson,

restraining Darren's arms above his head and preventing him from bringing them back down.

"Stop this, mon amour," James pleads in Darren's ear, holding him as tightly as he can. "You do not know what you do here!"

Darren twists his own body with a supernatural strength, and the force not only breaks the hold, it sends James flipping over onto his back. The top of the dais cracks his spine painfully. He begins to groan in pain, but the groan becomes a growl of determination and James forces himself to his feet.

Now it's him standing between the tip of Darren's spear and Consoné.

"Please put down the weapon, mon amour," James pleads with him again.

The muscles around Darren's right eye twitch, just a hair, and unlike when Lena spoke to him he actually seems to be focusing on James.

Darren swings the blunted end of the spear into James's face, bloodying his nose and staggering him several feet across the dais. James regains his footing quickly, shaking off the pain and impact of the blow. His expression becomes harder, more resolved.

"The man I have been with would never strike me," he says through the blood running over his lips. "You only show me this is not *my* Darren. I will not let whatever this is inside of you turn you into a killer, mon amour."

Darren turns the blunted end of the spear on him once more and thrusts it into James's face, snapping his head back and filling his mouth with blood.

But James refuses to go down.

Instead, he spits viscous red onto the dais and stares back at Darren with a fury none on the Sin du Jour line have ever seen the jovial young man display before.

"No!" he insists. "This will not be! Do you hear? Darren . . . listen to me, please . . . I did not come to America for money for my family. I did not even come here to cook. I left Senegal to be here what I could not be in my family's home. And to find what I have never had in my life. I came here to find you. I love you. I beg you now . . . come back to me."

As James speaks, Darren's jaw is seized by the same tremors he experienced in the trailer with Nikki. These, however, are more powerful and seem to begin spreading throughout his face and skull to the rest of his body. He stands there, frozen in place, trembling from head to toe, his every muscle seeming to strain to burst through his skin.

James can see the silent, agonizing turmoil inside him and how it's beginning to boil over.

"Please, mon amour," he presses. "Come back to me now. It is not too late. *Please.*"

Tears begin streaming from the corners of Darren's eyes, almost seeming to create steam as they hit his cheeks. Those eyes begin to clear, to soften, more closely resembling their original owner than they have in weeks.

The tip of the spear lowers, just an inch.

James's eyes widen hopefully.

"Good, Darren. Yes. Please. Just let go now. . . ."

The spear lowers another several inches, and a sound like a muffled word throws spittle from Darren's anguished mouth.

"What is it?" James askes. "Speak to me, mon amour. Tell me what has happened. . . ."

Darren tries to force more words out, but he can only sputter and retch. His hands quake spastically around the haft of the spear.

Steeling himself, James begins reaching out slowly to wrest it from him.

In the split second before his fingers touch Darren's closed fist, Consoné convulses and moans at James's heels.

The piece of Darren struggling to break through recedes like a child pulled under its bed by the monster there.

"Darren!" James yells, reaching for the spear, but it's too late.

Darren raises the weapon above his head and strikes.

The tip of the blade is aimed directly at James's heart.

It's less than half a foot away from piercing his chest when the entire world goes off its axis, the floor beneath their feet tilting more than seventy degrees. It throws the trajectory of Darren's strike off just enough that the blade of the spear skewers James's shoulder. He cries out and turns away just before they're both thrown from their feet.

Darren loses his grip on the spear, and trying to hold on only makes his fall wilder and even more off-kilter. His body flies several feet through the air before hitting the ground again and rolling from the top of the dais. He hits the onyx platform hard but manages to plant the soles of his feet and halt his inevitable slide.

The platform's sudden descent ceases just as suddenly.

Whether it was the jarring effect of the drop, or whether the effects of the magical shockwave are wearing off naturally, bodies all around Darren begin to stir and moan and occasionally cry for vengeance. He begins to stand carefully, to lean enough of his weight against the incline of the platform to keep him stable.

It turns out to be wasted effort. Darren never sees the object that collides with the back of his skull, but the force opens his head, sprays the onyx with blood, and floods his skull with a darkness that sees him crumpling to the platform and rolling down the incline until he loses momentum and sprawls.

Allensworth looks down at the unconscious body, Darren's blood still dripping from the churro crumb–filled mini-basket held in Allensworth's hand.

"The assassin is down!" he proclaims triumphantly. "Protect and attend to our new president!"

SKINNY DIPPING

For the last five minutes, Nikki has been pretending the bungee cord is the sinewy stalk of some vegetable, like broccoli, that's just been boiled too long. That's helping her ignore the truth, which is she's gnawing on old, dirty, greasy nylon. She doesn't know how long it will take that Darren robot to make his move; she only hopes she's moving fast enough. Spitting out the gag took a full minute all by itself.

But she's made progress. The length of cord closest to one of the bungee hooks is chewed almost to its center. Nikki imagines herself as a rat enthusiastically eating a corncob, nibbling fiercely at the dent she's made there. She applies the same laser focus that overtakes her in her pastry kitchen, meticulously crafting as close to perfection as humanly possible. It's still another five minutes before she feels the final tiny strands of cord against her tongue.

Nikki grips them with her jaw and yanks viciously, growling around them in determination and sheer will. The cord breaks and she immediately feels the tension around her wrists ease as one of the hooks loses its tether. She wriggles free of the bonds, spitting and trying not to retch or vomit all over the trailer floor.

Nikki unhooks her ankles and kicks free of the final bungee cords. Standing, she looks around frantically for a weapon, then realizes how absurd that is. She's not trying to physically overcome Darren; she just needs to tell someone.

She bolts for the door, pushing it up with both arms and leaping down from the back of the truck. She lands so hard, she rolls across the grass and has to recover her bearings before she can get back to her feet. The platform seems a million miles away, even if in reality it's only a short sprint from the tree line. Nikki makes a run for it.

She can sense something is already wrong even before she realizes it's far too deserted, too quiet. The party noises up there have all but ceased. She catches only a few scattered, unintelligible shouts. She can't see up onto the platform itself. Nikki stops running. She realizes she may be too late, or at the very least she *will* be too late to stop whatever's happening.

She moves her gaze around the shore, frantic, thoughts racing to come up with something, anything useful.

The only people still in sight are the robed mages surrounding the lake, using their silent, conjoined powers to keep the onyx platform hovering above the water.

"Oh, shit," Nikki says as she realizes what she's about to do.

She breaks into a run again, charging at the shore. Several yards from the first floating onyx step leading up to the platform, Nikki cuts a sudden left.

"Sorry, sorry, sorry, sorry, sorry!" she repeats over and over again, stopping only when she finally tackles the nearest robed mage.

Nikki feels a shock like a dog with an electric collar who wanders too far from their home yard. Then she feels the freezing water engulf her and the surprisingly frail figure to which she's clinging. They're separated almost immediately after they're both submerged. Nikki, in her heavy smock, begins sinking like a stone.

For several moments, she just stays there in the near-pitch darkness and total silence. Eventually, it occurs to her that she should swim back up to the surface. As Nikki prepares to kick her feet and spread her arms, the silence and the darkness are both obliterated by the entire front edge of the onyx platform crashing down through the water.

A flood of moonlight blinds her and a force unlike anything she's ever felt rushes beneath her and lifts her up through the water. She feels cool air at first grasping her skin then rushing around her. Weightlessness gives way to the harshness of gravity and she's pulled back down to Earth. Nikki collides with solid ground, and all the oxygen seems to leave her body at once.

When she can breathe (read: "cough up water") and see again, Nikki realizes she's somehow been knocked all the way back onto shore. She's also surrounded by inauguration party guests, some sprawled out on the grass around her, and others crawling back up from the water.

She looks up. The onyx platform is tilted on its axis, several yards of it submerged in the water in front of her. Tents have collapsed. Tables and chairs are overturned. There isn't a person or creature left standing.

All she can do is say again, helplessly, "Sorry."

STAND AND DELIVER

Lena is dreaming of the shade tree she occupied for much of her and Darren's high school career. It sprouted from a small patch of grass lined with concrete curb facing the teacher's parking lot at the northernmost tip of the school. It was a virtual student no-man's-land, and that's why she and Darren liked it. Lena would spend every lunch and free period there, reading Octavia Butler and Magda Szabó (one of her personal heroes) and Ursula Le Guin.

She wakes up to the heavy lines of Bronko's face, all of them contorted in concern. He's leaning over her, one hand gently cupping her right shoulder. There's pain in her head, pain in her jaw, and a constant throbbing of blood in her right cheek. She can feel the bandage there seeping wetly, the alien sensation of the stitches woven in and out of her flesh underneath it.

She realizes she's lying on Bronko's couch, back in his office at Sin du Jour. She barely remembers the trip back or the medical treatment after she regained consciousness. They must have given her some heavy drugs at the scene.

"Darren?" she asks immediately, groggily. "James?"

"James took a very large blade clean through one shoulder. It'll heal; he'll just have that arm slung up for a goodly while. Vargas is alive. He's being kept sedated and under guard by the *Sceadu*. It's clear he was possessed by somethin', *is* possessed by somethin', some kind of evil that's taken root right in his soul. I called White Horse, interrupted his teaching sabbatical, told him what went down. He agrees. He's on his way back. Now, I have no doubt he'll be able to cleanse Vargas of whatever's taken hold. He'll be okay, Tarr."

"'Okay' is a relative concept when it comes to people."

Bronko nods. "It surely is. Fortunately, Vargas has people like you and James close to him. And he's got me and the line and the staff. There'll be fallout, external and internal. But we'll fix it. Okay?"

"Yes, Chef. What about the others?"

"Jett made it back. Dorsky, Pacific, and Mo are still unaccounted for. Sure enough the Secret Service has them."

Lena sits up in alarm. "You seem awful damn calm about it, Chef."

"Yeah, well, we got one thing going in our favor."

"What could that possibly be?"

"You know how you saw America's new president blown to synthetic chunks and a live gremlin explode from his chest?"

"Yeah."

"Well, no one else does. No one else saw it."

"What?"

"Just like I said. They tape-delayed the broadcast, sent out some kind of glamour. As for the folks who were there live, well, there are ways to erase that memory. And if they miss a few hundred, even a few thousand, who's going to pay any mind to a story like that?"

Lena is stunned. "So, nothing happened?"

"Close enough. And if it didn't, then there's no reason to hold our people."

"Yeah, unless they shoot them and bury them for the convenience of it."

Bronko is resolute. "We'll get them back."

Lena is going to argue, but then another thought, one that rides a high and bloody wave of rage, crashes over her brain.

Lena stands, carefully, readjusting to having her feet under her again.

"Where's Ritter?" she asks him once she has her bearings.

"He's here. I called everybody in to catch 'em up on the events of the evening."

Lena nods, turning and walking toward the office door.

"Hey there!" he calls after her. "You okay, Tarr?"

"Relatively," she says without stopping or looking back.

The halls outside Bronko's office look foreign and strange to her. Lena isn't sure if it's the meds they gave her for her face, or being knocked unconscious, or if the past twelve hours crossed some kind of invisible line in her psyche from which there's no return.

She finds Ritter in the main kitchen, by himself, eating leftover sushi Tenryu made for the staff's last family meal. When he sees her enter the kitchen, he chews and swallows his last piece of makizushi quickly, setting the plastic container aside.

"How deep is that?" he asks, waving four fingertips over the patch of his cheek where, on Lena's face, the seeping bandage is taped.

"One more scar," she says without emotion, navigating the grid of stainless steel islands to meet him.

Ritter stands a little straighter, ready to embrace her, ready to give her whatever she needs.

Lena closes the remaining gap between them in three quick strides and then punches Ritter in the face.

It doesn't rock him, but it does sting all the way to the tips of his ears and bloody his nose. Lena puts more power behind the second punch, this one landing against his jaw and actually wobbling him a little.

Ritter stares down at her in abject surprise, but he

makes no move to fight back or even defend himself.

The third time Lena rears back to strike him, she turns deeper into it than she yet has, and when the blow comes around, it runs straight through his chin with adrenaline-fueled force. Ritter loses a split second of time and drops to his right knee, drunkenly leaning to one side until his shoulder pressing against a refrigerator stops him.

He shakes his head viciously in his attempt to vent the fog between his ears. The blood from his nose has run over his lips and is dripping from his chin onto his plain black T-shirt.

Lena stands over him with her fists clenched tightly at her side, the knuckles of her right hand split, his blood mingling with hers in those small wounds. There's unfiltered rage filling her eyes to their barest corners, and she's breathing through a layer of tearful snot and spittle.

"You tell me the truth now!" she demands, a powerful fury in her voice even if it is shaken with sorrow. "I don't want any of your brooding alpha-male bullshit, d'you hear me? You tell me what happened with Darren and you and Allensworth and you tell me all of it! I want to know what you fucking did to Darren and why!"

"It wasn't me who did that to him," Ritter whispers, haunted, unable to look up at her.

Lena kicks him sharply in the knee that isn't pasted to the kitchen floor.

Ritter grimaces, clasping his hands over the offended kneecap. "Goddammit, Lena!"

"The truth, I said!"

Ritter sighs, letting his head fall back none too gently against the stainless steel door of the fridge. "It wasn't me who did that to him, but I sent him there. I sent him to whoever or whatever did it."

Lena shakes her head, more tears filling her eyes. "Why . . . Why would you do that? Why would you *ever* do that? That doesn't make any sense!"

"I didn't know what he was walking into," Ritter insists. "Allensworth gave me an address. That's all."

"So, you're that wannabe underworld dictator's boy now, is that it?"

Ritter doesn't answer at first. He slumps down onto his ass, back pressed into the refrigerator.

"I used to, uh . . . I used to hunt witches for a living," he begins, and he laughs suddenly, absurdly, laughter that mutates in the barest sliver of a second into tears.

He quickly swallows those back as well.

"I didn't ask for your fucking backstory, Ritter."

"You want to know why. This is why. I joined WET. 'Witchcraft Enforcement Team,'" he enunciates slowly and with bitter irony. "It was Allensworth's brainchild. It was supposed to be elite shit, hunting rogue magic-users. Dangerous people using out-of-control powers to do very bad shit. The worst of the worst. They had to be not just tracked down and stopped but destroyed. That was the mandate."

He falls quiet again.

"And?" Lena presses, though it's less impatient than before. Her stomach is starting to twist.

"It was all bullshit," Ritter admits, genuine pain registering in every contour of his face. "It was just Allensworth's never-ending control trip. He wanted every human magic-user in the fucking world to answer to him solely. He created a coven-only structure to make sure. Anyone who didn't join . . . they ran or they disappeared. The women we hunted down . . . they were just scared. Jesus, if they even were women. A lot of them were just girls, barely old enough to . . ."

"What did you do?" Lena asks, though the answer is obvious, inescapable.

His voice becomes very far away. "We burned them. All of them. High-tech thermite. Next-generation shit. Quick and horrible. We burned them all alive."

Lena can't decide whether she wants to hit him again or throw up all over him.

"I couldn't take it anymore," he continues, near tears himself again. "I wanted out. Allensworth let me go, but only because he needed someone doing this job. That was our deal. My brother, Marcus, stayed behind. He finally cracked. He's more . . . impulsive than me. He just ran. Allensworth found him. He was going to take Marcus out. Allensworth offered me a deal. He wanted Darren. He didn't say why or for what. He just told me to send him to that brownstone and stay out of it."

"And what did you think would happen?" Lena asks, even more disgusted.

"I thought Allensworth would give the kid a choice. Because that's what he does. He never . . . *forces* you to do anything. You know? At least, he didn't before this. He offers you a simple choice, and he weights the one he wants you to make so heavy, you can't go any other way. I hoped Darren would be smarter than me. Stronger than me."

"Right. Because you turned him into a tough guy."

Ritter finally looks up at her. There's more emotion in his face than Lena has ever seen displayed there.

"Because he was brave enough to ask me for help," he says. "I've never been that strong."

"You piece of shit," Lena hisses at him.

There's a magnetic strip bolted above the station behind her. The blades of a dozen kitchen knives are held, suspended, to it. Lena reaches for the largest butcher's knife, snatching it down and holding its tip inches from Ritter's face, menacingly.

"If you *ever* come near me, Darren, or anyone on my

line again, I will fucking kill you."

Ritter doesn't even see the blade. He stares straight past it at her face.

There isn't any doubting her sincerity in that moment.

"I know you're a badass kung fu half-wizard mercenary or whatever the fuck, but I will find a way. I will wait until you're sleeping and I will slit your goddamn throat. Do you understand me?"

Ritter nods.

Lena drops the knife. It clatters on the kitchen floor between them, ringing out sharply.

She turns and strides away. Ten feet from the kitchen entrance, Lena breaks into a run, knowing if she doesn't, the tears will seize her before she can make it out.

Ritter's left sitting there alone, staring at the knife on the floor. All the light in the kitchen seems to be held there in the flat of the blade. It shines like edged enlightenment, bright enough to make him close his eyes when he stares at its center too intently.

Ritter finds, in that moment, he prefers the darkness.

It's much, much easier.

ACKNOWLEDGMENTS

When I first pitched my overly ambitious seven-novella concept for Sin du Jour, I quite honestly never expected to see book three released, let alone make it to book number five. It's a helluva thing, and I still firmly believe it wouldn't have happened without Tor.com Publishing creating such a unique home for projects like these. I owe the team behind Tor.com Publishing all my gratitude, chief among them my editor and eternal champion (damn right in the Michael Moorcock sense), Lee Harris, and associate publisher, Irene Gallo. I also want to thank Mordicai Knode and Katharine Duckett, who've strived tirelessly to get the word out about the series, and Carl Engle-Laird, who always provides unending support in whatever form it's needed. Peter Lutjen, whose cover design just gets more epic with each book, and *Greedy Pig*'s copyeditor, Richard Shealy. I feel genuinely privileged to have a group of professionals with their combined talents elevating my work. I always owe gratitude to the folks in my own life who prop up me and my writing as needed. My agent and the best-dressed man in publishing, Dong-Won Song, who is the literary representation equivalent of a Hattori Hanzō sword. My fiancée, Nikki, my toughest critic and fiercest supporter. My mother, Barbara, the single most tireless champion of my books. Finally, my thanks to you, the constant reader of Sin du Jour. You're the most important person in my little made-up universe, because you keep the lights on. Thank you.

About the Author

Photograph by Earl Newton

MATT WALLACE is the author of *The Next Fix*, *The Failed Cities*, and his other novella series, Slingers. He's also penned more than one hundred short stories, a few of which have won awards and been nominated for others, in addition to writing for film and television. In his youth he traveled the world as a professional wrestler and unarmed combat and self-defense instructor before retiring to write full-time.

He now resides in Los Angeles with the love of his life and inspiration for Sin du Jour's resident pastry chef.

TOR·COM

**Science fiction. Fantasy. The universe.
And related subjects.**

*

More than just a publisher's website, *Tor.com*
is a venue for **original fiction, comics,** and
discussion of the entire field of SF and fantasy,
in all media and from all sources. Visit our site
today—and join the conversation yourself.